This little baby

It explained exactly why his crooning and shushing and swaying had been so effective, earlier today. He'd had practice. Recent practice, and a lot of it.

"You'd better come in," he said. "I think she's going to sleep. You're not catching her at the best time. I wish you could see her smiling, the way she's been doing the past month."

"It's a girl?"

"Yes."

Dev had just mentioned she'd been smiling for the past month, and Jodie had enough nieces and nephews that she knew when smiling happened— six weeks or so. This baby had to be about ten weeks old.

Do the math, Jodie, do the math. Nine months plus two and a half equals almost a year. When you were busy "getting the old crush out of your system" last fall, the mother of Dev's baby must already have been pregnant...

But where was the mother now? *Who* was the mother?

Dear Reader,

As any writer will tell you, some books are harder to write than others. This was one of those times when it all came together so clearly. I found myself with a gutsy heroine facing enormous challenges and a miracle or two, a hero who does the right thing but hasn't yet learned what his heart really wants, and a loving family who sometimes make the wrong choices for the best of reasons, and there was the story.

Even so, there were some surprises as I wrote. Jodie's career as a teacher of riding became more important than I thought it would be. It draws on all the experience I'm gaining from being involved with my daughter's passion for horses. The nighttime scene between Devlin and Jodie on their way back from an evening out wrote itself onto the page in a way I hadn't planned, but as soon as it was there I knew it was right.

I hope this book makes you laugh and cry, and that you're as eager for Jodie and Dev to find the path to their own happiness as I was.

Lilian Darcy

THE MOMMY MIRACLE

LILIAN DARCY

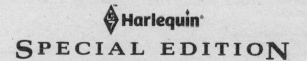

Harlequin®

SPECIAL EDITION

Recycling programs
for this product may
not exist in your area.

ISBN-13: 978-0-373-65616-5

THE MOMMY MIRACLE

Printed in U.S.A.

LILIAN DARCY

has written nearly eighty books for Silhouette Romance, Silhouette Special Edition and Harlequin Medical Romance (Prescription Romance). Happily married, with four active children and a very patient cat, she enjoys keeping busy and could probably fill several more lifetimes with the things she likes to do—including cooking, gardening, quilting, drawing and traveling. She currently lives in Australia, but travels to the United States as often as possible to visit family. Lilian loves to hear from readers. You can write to her at P.O. Box 532, Jamison P.O., Macquarie ACT 2614, Australia, or email her at lilian@liliandarcy.com.

Chapter One

"I don't think she's ready yet." The words floated up through Jodie's open bedroom window from the back deck.

"Oh, I agree! She's not!"

No one in the Palmer family ever thought Jodie was ready. She sat on her bed, struggling to raise her left arm high enough to push her hand through the strap on her summery, sparkly, brand-new tank top. The hand wouldn't go, which meant she couldn't start the long journey down the stairs to join the Fourth of July family barbecue as the—not her idea—guest of honor.

She pushed again, the feeble muscle refusing to obey the muddy signal from her brain. It was noon; time for everyone to start arriving. "So I guess they're right. I'm not ready," she muttered, but she knew this wasn't what her sister Lisa's comment had meant.

It had meant Not Ready, capital *N*, capital *R*, and

during Jodie's twenty-nine years had covered everything from her learning the shocking truth about the Easter Bunny at the age of seven, to going out on her first date at fifteen. She vaguely remembered from last summer, about a hundred years ago, that Elin had even questioned her readiness to see Orlando Bloom's wedding photos in a magazine—and, admittedly, she had been a little envious of the bride.

What wasn't she ready for this time?

It could be anything. Going back to work?

Well, yes, she knew she wouldn't be doing that for a while, since she managed and taught at a riding barn for a living and spent hours in the saddle every week at Oakbank Stables.

Reading the police report on the accident scene? Might never be ready for that one. Fixing her own coffee? Wrong, sisters. She'd been practicing in rehab and, not to sound arrogant or anything, she was *dynamite* when it came to spooning the granules out of the jar.

"Guys?" she called out to her sisters. "Can I have some help up here?"

From down on the deck she heard an exclamation, voices, the scrape of chairs. Lisa and Elin both appeared half a minute later, flinging the bedroom door back on its hinges with a slam, wearing frightened looks to complement their red-white-and-blue patriotic earrings.

"It's okay," she told them. "You can put the defibrillator down and cancel the 911 call. I just can't get my arm into this top, that's all, and I know people will start arriving any second."

"Maddy and John just drove up," Lisa confirmed. "And Devlin was right behind them."

"Devlin's coming?" Jodie's heart bumped sideways against her ribs. Dev. Every time she saw Dev...

There was an odd little silence. Possibly there was. It ended so quickly that she wasn't even sure if it had happened.

"He's been so great, hasn't he?" Lisa said brightly. "How many times did he go in to see you, while you were in the hospital?"

"You tell me," Jodie joked. "I was unconscious for most of them."

"Do you remember anything from that time?" Elin asked, hesitant. At forty, she was the eldest of the four Palmer girls, and managed to be both the bossiest and the most nurturing at the same time. "The doctors said you might retain some memories, even from when you weren't responsive."

She and Lisa both stood there waiting for her reply, each almost holding their breath. Jodie fought a bad-tempered impulse to yell at them to stop the heck worrying about her so much!

Instead she said carefully, "I wouldn't call them memories...."

"No...?" prompted Lisa.

"But let's not talk about it now. Help me downstairs. I'm so slow. My brain sends the instructions but bits of my body don't respond. I'm thrilled I managed to get into the jeans."

Thirty-eight-year-old Lisa, sister number two, hugged Jodie suddenly with a warm, tight squeeze, and planted a smacking kiss on her cheek. Of the four Palmer girls, she and Jodie were physically the most alike, blonde and athletic, outdoorsy and lean. Lisa liked tennis and the beach and it had started to show in her tanned skin. She didn't take care of it the way she should. Hugging her back, Jodie decided she'd have to give Lisa a sisterly lecture about that, soon, because Palmer overprotectiveness could cut both ways.

The slight, strange tension in the room seemed to have gone, chased by the hug. "Honey, forget slow, we're just so happy you're okay," Lisa said. "Talking. Walking. Getting better every day. *Home.*"

"I know." Jodie blinked back sudden tears as they let each other go. "Me, too."

Devlin Browne was standing on the deck when she reached it, his dark hair showing reddish glints in the sun, his body tall and strong; there was no evidence of the accident that had injured the two of them in such different ways, nine months ago. He grinned at the sight of her, from behind his sunglasses. "Look at you!" She wished she could see the expression in his blue eyes. He ran his life with such quiet confidence and certainty. She loved that about him, wished right now that some of his qualities would rub off on her.

"Yeah," she drawled in reply, "all the grace of a ballerina."

With a walking frame for a dance partner. The doctors and therapists had promised that if she worked hard, she'd be rid of it soon. She planned to astonish them with her progress.

"Don't knock it," Dev said. "Compared to how you were even a week ago."

"I know. I'm not knocking it, believe me." She felt so self-conscious in his presence, so aware of the strong length of his body. Nine months and more since those three explosive nights of lovemaking, but to her they felt like yesterday. The way their bodies seemed to fit together so perfectly. The smell of him, warm and fresh and male. The words he'd whispered to her in the dark, naked and blunt and charged with sensual heat. Did he ever think about it?

Lisa helped her to sit down and took away the frame, while Elin handed her an ice-cold glass of tropical juice. The deck was dappled with sun and shade, and there was a breeze. It was a perfect day. Dev pulled up an Adirondack chair to sit beside her. He leaned against the wooden seat-back, casually stretched his arms. But his mood wasn't as casual as he wanted her to think. His gaze seemed intently focused behind those concealing sunglasses, and she didn't know if his sitting so close was significant.

Were they dating?

Could she ask?

Um, excuse me, Dev, I was in a coma for nearly eight months, and rehab since. Can you just catch me up on the current status of our relationship?

A thought struck her. That Not Ready comment of Lisa's a few minutes ago…

Not Ready to hear that Dev had moved on to someone else?

But she didn't have time to examine the cold pit that opened deep in her stomach at this idea. There shouldn't be a pit! He'd been up front with her nine months ago. "I have nothing to offer, Jodie," he'd said. "I'm only here until Dad is ready to go back to work. My career is in New York, it's pretty full-on, no room for commitment, and I'm not looking for it. I really like being with you, but if you're interested in something long-term, it's not with me."

How did a woman respond to something like that? She knew Dev had said it out of innate honesty and goodness of heart. He wasn't the kind of man who promised what he couldn't deliver, or tricked a woman into bed with sweet-talking lies. He called it how he saw it, and when he laid his cards on the table, he laid them straight.

Nine months ago he'd been all about the short term, about saying goodbye when it was over, with a big grin, warm wishes and no regrets for either of them, yet now he was sitting beside her, searching her face, examining the set of her shoulders as if he cared that she might not be coping.

Which she wasn't, fully.

Everything was happening too fast. Dev stood up to greet Lisa's husband. Mom and Dad came out from the kitchen, Dad in full male barbecue armor, with plastic apron and an impressive weaponry of implements. The front doorbell rang and Elin went to answer it.

And sister number three—Maddy—and her husband, John, were here, having at last managed to negotiate the trip from their car. They'd come around the side of the house and climbed the steps to the deck carrying two bulging diaper bags, some kind of squishy portable baby gym and a baby in a carrier.

Their baby. Their little girl. Tiny. Just a few weeks old. Jodie hadn't even known Maddy was pregnant. She'd only been told about baby Lucy after she was born—another questionable instance of Not Ready— and hadn't seen her yet, because Maddy and John lived in Cincinnati, two hours from Leighville, the Palmer family's Southern Ohio hometown.

"Oh, she's asleep!" Mom crooned. "Oh, what an angel! She already looks so much bigger than she did two weeks ago."

"Can we put her somewhere quiet?" Maddy asked.

But it was too late. The baby began to waken, stretching her little body in the cramped space of the car carrier and letting out a keening cry.

"Oh, she needs a feed," Maddy said. "Where shall I go?"

"Not here," Dad said. He was a traditional man, with a passion for woodworking and gadgetry. In his world, feeding and diaper changes didn't belong in the same space as a barbecue.

"You wouldn't believe how difficult it was just to get here, all the gear we had to bring. John, can you set up some pillows for me in...? Oh, where!"

"My room," Jodie said quickly. "There's a heap of pillows, and fresh flowers, and a rocking chair."

"Oops, I'm going to have to change her first...." But John had already gone to ready the room. Maddy held Lucy with the baby's legs awkwardly dangling and her little face screwed up as she screamed, and looked around for the diaper bag. "She's in a mess. Oh, I'm not good at any of this yet! Where's the monitor? We'll need it if she naps. I have no idea if she will. And when she cries like this... First baby at thirty-six, people do say it's harder."

"Here, don't worry, it's fine." Of all people, it was Dev who stepped forward and took the crying baby. He cradled her against his shoulder and commenced a kind of rocking sway and a rhythmic soothing sound. "Shh-sh, shh-sh, it's okay, Mommy's coming in a minute, shh-sh, shh-sh." Jodie felt a strange, unwanted tingling in her breasts and a familiar yearning in her heart. Why did he do this to her when she tried so hard to stay sensible? How could he possibly look so confident and so good, holding a poop-stained baby? Why was he still in Ohio, and not back in New York?

She had a vivid flashback, suddenly, to the first night

they'd made love. Bed on the first date. You weren't supposed to do that, if you were a female with a warm heart, but of course it hadn't felt like the first date. She'd known Dev since she was sixteen, and she'd responded to him with half a lifetime of pent-up feeling—to his hands so right on her body, to his voice so familiar in her ear.

"Thank you, Dev!" Maddy unzipped the diaper bag and rummaged around inside. She didn't seem surprised that Devlin had taken control, but Jodie was.

Not about the control, but about the thing he was in control *of.* If you were talking legal contracts or high finance or building plans, team sports, political wrangling, then, yes, Devlin Browne could take control in a heartbeat. Would always take control. But when it was a *baby?*

What did he know about babies?

He doesn't even want kids.

The thought came out of nowhere, one of the memories from before the accident that her brain threw out apparently at random. "Did I have amnesia?" Jodie had asked at one point.

"Not like in the movies," they—her doctors and therapists—had said. "But of course there are some gaps. Many of them you'll eventually fill in. Some you never will."

"Like the accident itself?"

"Yes, it's quite probable you'll never remember that."

But she remembered that Dev didn't want kids.

How did she remember that?

She searched her mind, watching him as he gently bounced the baby on his shoulder. He wore jeans and a gray polo shirt with black trim, filling the clothing with a body honed by running and wilderness sports. The fabric of the jeans pulled tightly across his thighs, and the sleeve-band of the polo shirt was tight, too. There was some impressive muscle mass there, and Jodie's fingers remembered it, even while she was trying to remember the other thing—the thing about him not wanting kids.

If he didn't want kids, how could he school all that male strength into the tender touch and soft rhythm needed to soothe a newborn baby? When Maddy was ready, he handed Lucy over to her, and casually warned, "Watch the wet patch on her back."

But he didn't want any of his own...

Okay, it was over dinner, she remembered. They'd been out together—and slept together, heaven help her—three times since his temporary return to Leigh-ville. As far as Jodie's family were concerned, she and Dev had only been dipping their toes in the waters of the great big dating lake.

To her, though, it immediately felt deeper. She'd had a major crush on him at sixteen when he'd briefly dated one of her good friends before he—Dev—had left for college in Chicago a couple of months later. Turned out the crush had never really gone away.

She couldn't track back to how the subject of kids had come up that night. Maybe something to do with his restless lifestyle. He was based in New York these days, but his work in international law took him all over the world—three months in London, a summer in Prague. He'd only come home for a couple of months last fall to take over his father's small-town legal practice on a temporary basis while Mac Browne had heart surgery.

Okay, so she might possibly have asked Dev, over their meal, if he ever intended to settle down.

He'd probably said no, he didn't. The I-have-nothing-to-offer thing, again.

And then he'd definitely—twenty seconds or five minutes later—said that he didn't want kids. Fatherhood didn't fit with his plans.

Which was fine, she'd thought, because he was only in town for a short while, and she'd only gone into this dating thing so she could finally get a thirteen-year crush well and truly out of her system and then wave him goodbye. A big grin, and no regrets.

Or not.

If I sleep with him, he'll break my heart when he leaves, she'd thought back then. *And if I don't sleep with him, he'll* still *break my heart when he leaves....*

But that was last October, and he was still here. The accident would explain part of it. October eighth, the two of them driving home after dark from date number four, a fall hike in Hocking Hills followed by dinner, when a driver in an oncoming car had lost control around a bend. Devlin had broken his leg in three places and had a permanent metal plate in there, but he didn't even walk with a limp at this point, so shouldn't he be safely back in New York or in a hotel room in Geneva by now?

Instead he was standing here on her parents' summer deck sharing a joke with her dad, throwing up his head when he laughed, shirt fabric pulling across his broad shoulders when he raised a beer can to his lips, reminding her far too strongly that she hadn't remotely gotten the crush out of her system last fall, or during the nine months of coma and rehab since.

He'd come to visit her in the hospital five times since she'd woken up, seen her at her most vulnerable, in tears and struggling to move and speak, fighting her own uncooperative body. He'd been so supportive, but cautious at the same time, never talking about anything too personal, and she had no idea what it all meant. Her brain still felt scrambled, tired, and life was a jigsaw puzzle with too many pieces missing.

"Is she out here? How is she?" This was Jodie's Aunt Stephanie, following Elin out to the deck. Seemed as if *everyone* had been invited today. Jodie began to feel overwhelmed and more than a little tired. She'd been discharged from the nearby rehab unit yesterday, and would still be attending day therapy sessions there for a while. She'd spent just one night, so far, in her own precious bed.

"Jodie…!" Aunt Stephanie said, and leaned down to hug her.

Dad put hot dogs and burgers and steaks onto the barbecue grill. Lisa brought out bowls of salad. Lisa's husband, Chris, took a soccer ball onto the grass beyond the deck and began kicking it back and forth with a handful of kids. Everyone talked and laughed and caught up on family news.

Maddy came down with Lucy wide awake and contentedly milk-filled in her arms, and Jodie asked her on an impulse, "Can I have a hold? If you put a pillow under my left arm, so I don't have to use any muscle?"

She felt a strange yearning and a rush of emotion that she didn't remember feeling for her other nieces and nephews when they were newborn. Well, she'd only been in her early twenties then, not ready to think about babies. Lisa's youngest was seven years old.

"Do you want to, honey?" Mom asked, in a slightly odd voice. "Hold her?"

"Yes, didn't I just ask?"

"Quick, someone grab a pillow from the couch,"

Mom ordered urgently, as if baby Lucy were a grenade with the pin pulled and would explode if Jodie didn't have her nestled on a pillow in the next five seconds.

"John?" Maddy said, in the same tone.

"Coming right up." He ran so fast for the pillow Jodie expected him to come back breathless.

Sheesh, she thought, *I could probably ask for a metallic gold European sports car convertible with red leather seats right now, and there'd be one in the driveway by the end of the afternoon. You know, I should definitely go for that...*

Maddy stuffed the pillow between the arm of the chair and Jodie's elbow. "Now, just cradle her head here, Jodie. If you're not sure about this…"

"C'mon, Maddy, lighten up. I've held babies before. I've been holding them for years." Elin's eldest two were in their midteens.

"Yeah, but this is *my* baby," Maddy joked, in a slightly wobbly voice.

Okay, so it was a new-mother thing. Fair enough.

But there was that feeling in the air again, everyone seeming to hold their breath, everyone watching Jodie a little too closely. Mom, Lisa, Dev. Dev, especially, his body held so still he could have been made of bronze.

The accident. The coma. That was why.

When she was one hundred percent fit and well, would they finally stop?

"Shouldn't be such a fuss, should it?" Dad muttered from behind the barrier of the barbecue grill. No one took any notice.

Jodie held the baby, smelled the sweet, milky smell of her breath, the nutty scent of her pink baby scalp covered in a swirl of downy dark hair, and the hint of lavender in her stretchy cotton dress, from the special baby laundry detergent. Oh, she was so sweet, just adorable, and if everyone was staring at the two of them, well, that was fine and normal. It was one of the *rightest* sights in the world, a person tenderly holding a newborn child.

"Oh, you sweet, precious thing," she crooned. "Thank you for not crying for your auntie, little darling."

She bent forward and planted a kiss on the silky hair, and took in those sweet scents again, close to tears. As she straightened again, she could smell onions frying, too, the aroma unusually intense and satisfying, as if she'd never smelled frying onions before. Sometimes her brain reacted this way, since coming out of the coma. It was as if all her senses had been reborn.

And then suddenly they hit overload, like little Lucy hitting overload when she was due for her nap.

"Can you have her, Maddy? My arms are getting tired."

"You did great," Maddy said, and too many people echoed the praise. Dev growled it half under his breath.

But maybe they were right. She felt wiped. Dev leaned toward her. "Are you okay?"

"Need some lunch."

"Just that?"

"Well, tired…"

Baby Lucy yawned on her behalf, and Maddy murmured something about taking her upstairs.

"To Jodie's room," Mom said quickly. "Not in—"

"No, I know," Maddy answered, already halfway inside.

"But I definitely need lunch," Jodie admitted.

"Sit," Dev ordered. "I'll grab whatever you want." There was a tiny beat of hesitation. "You did great with the baby."

"So did you."

"Uh, yeah." A quick breath. "Hot dog with everything?"

"Please!" She managed the hot dog, covered in bright red ketchup and heaped with those delicious onions, managed replies to various questions from family members, and to a comment on the kids' soccer game from Dev, managed probably another half hour of sitting there—Maddy had come back downstairs with the baby monitor in her hand—and then she just couldn't hold it together, couldn't pretend anymore, guest of honor or not, and Dev said, "You need to rest. Right now."

Mom didn't quite get it. "Oh, but Devlin, it's her party! We've barely started!"

"Take a look at her."

Jodie tried to say, "I'm fine," but it came out on a croak.

"You're right, Devlin," Mom said. "Jodie, let's take you upstairs."

"But Lucy's asleep on her bed," Maddy said.

"Couch is okay," Jodie replied. "Nice to hear everyone talking." She joked, "I mean, it is my party."

"Here," said Dev, the way he'd said it to Maddy over an hour ago, about baby Lucy. He helped her up and she leaned on him, and he smelled to her baby-new nose like pine woods and warm grain and sizzling steak. He didn't pass her the walking frame, just said, "Don't worry, I've got you," and she found that he did. He was so much better than the frame, so much more solid and warm, with his chest shoring up her shoulder and his chin grazing her hair. Her heart wanted to stay this close to him for hours, but the rest of her body wouldn't cooperate.

They reached the couch and he plumped up the

silk-covered cushions, grabbed the unfinished hand-stitched quilt top her mother was working on, tucked it around her like a three-hundred thread-count cotton sheet and ordered, "Rest."

"I will."

"I'll leave your frame here within reach, if you need to get up."

"Thank you, Dev." She'd already closed her eyes, so she wasn't sure that he'd touched her. She thought he had, with the brush of his fingertips over her hair, but maybe it was just a drift of air from his movement. She didn't want to open her eyes to find out, or to discover he'd gone. Touch or air, she could feel it to her bones.

He must have gone. She hadn't heard his footsteps on the carpet, but now there was that sense of quiet.

Sleepy quiet.

In the kitchen, making coffee and cutting cake, Elin said, in a voice that wasn't nearly as soft as she thought, "I don't think she was ready for this many people so soon."

"It's just family," answered Lisa.

"It's a big family," Maddy pointed out.

"Mom wanted a celebration for her coming home." Lisa again.

"We should have waited a week or two for that." Elin.

"But by then…" Maddy.

"I know. I know." Elin sighed.

Jodie shut all of it out, the way she'd learned to shut out the noise and the interruptions in the hospital and rehab unit, and drifted into sleep. When she woke up again, her sisters were still in the kitchen.

No, she amended to herself, in the kitchen *again*.

They were cleaning up this time, and the way they were talking made it clear that most people had gone, including Maddy, Lucy and John. She must have slept for a couple of hours, and the house had grown hotter with windows and deck doors open. Was Dev still here? She could hear the vigorous, metallic sound of Dad cleaning off the barbecue out on the deck, and Elin and Chris's kids still playing in the yard, but no Dev.

She felt refreshed but stiff-limbed. Here was the walking frame within reach, just as Dev had promised. She twisted to a sitting position, inched forward on the couch and pulled herself up, automatically comparing her strength to yesterday, and a week ago, and a week before that.

Better.

I'm getting better.

Her therapists had told her it would come with work and so far today she hadn't done any work, just a few range of motion exercises for her hands and arms this morning.

Time for a walk.

She called out to her sisters in the kitchen, to tell them what she was doing, and Elin appeared. "You're sure?"

"I'm supposed to, now, as much as I feel like. I'll only go around the block."

"Need company?"

"No!" It came out a little more sharply than she'd intended.

The Not Ready stuff drove her crazy. It had been driving her crazy for years.

Not ready to go for a walk on her own, in her own street, at three-thirty in the afternoon on the Fourth of July? Come on!

She'd once said to her three big sisters, long ago, "I'm littler 'n you *now,* but watch out 'cause I'm getting bigger!" and somehow she was still insisting on that message, twenty-something years later, even though, thanks to a serious childhood illness at the age of five that had apparently scared the pants off of the entire family permanently, she never had caught up to them size-wise and was the smallest and shortest at size 4 and five foot three. But she didn't need the level of protectiveness they and her mother gave her. Why couldn't they see it?

Dad seemed to have an inkling, but he rarely interfered. She remembered just a handful of times. "Let her have horse-riding lessons, Barbara, for heck's sake!" he'd said to Mom when Jodie was seven. "It'll make her stronger." And then ten years later, "If she wants to work with horses as a career, then she should. She should follow her heart."

"No, thanks," she repeated to Elin more gently, because anger wasn't the way to go. "Send out a search party if I'm not back in forty-five minutes or so, okay? And I have my phone. You think anyone in Leighville is going to look the other way if they find someone collapsed on the sidewalk in front of their house?"

"You sure?"

"I'm sure, Elin. You can help me down the front steps, is all."

It felt so good, once Elin had gone back inside. To be on her own, but not alone in a hospital rehab bed. To be out in the warm, fresh day, with no one watching over her, or telling her, "Yes! You can do it!" with far too much encouragement and enthusiasm, every time she put one step in front of another.

I could walk for miles!

No, okay, not *miles*, let's be realistic, here.

But maybe more than just around the block. She had

the frame for support. It would be slow going, concentration still required for every step, and the afternoon heat had grown sticky, but she'd never been a quitter. There'd be a garden wall or park bench to sit on if she was tired. There were all those neighbors looking out for her, knowing about the accident and that she had just come home.

She could walk to Dev's.

Or rather, Dev's parents'. He'd mentioned today that he was living there for the time being, just a throwaway line that she hadn't thought about at the time because she'd been fighting the sense of fatigue and overload, but now it came back to her.

And it didn't make sense.

Why was Dev living at his parents' place, even as a temporary thing? Jodie was living with hers because of the accident, but that was different. Why was he still here in Leighville at all, when she had such a strong memory from nine months ago, of his insistence that he planned to return to New York as soon as he could?

It had something to do with her, with the accident, she was sure of it, and if her family had somehow roped him into the whole let's-protect-Jodie-till-she-can't-breathe-on-her-own scenario, then damn it, he had to be stopped. He had to be told.

I don't need it, Devlin. I don't want it. Not from you or from anyone else.

She was definitely walking to Dev's, and they were going to talk.

Chapter Two

"Shh-sh," Dev crooned, bouncing the baby gently against his shoulder. "Shh-sh."

It did no good. His rhythmic sway and soothing sounds had had more success with baby Lucy today than they were having now with his own child, in his own house. He'd heard her screaming as he came up the front path, and the sitter had met him at the door, looking harassed and more than ready to go home.

"I'm sorry, Mr. Browne, she just won't settle."

He'd taken the baby, paid the sitter, tried everything he knew in the hour since, but DJ was still crying. He knew from experience—over two months of it, since she'd come home from the hospital—that she would settle eventually, that it wasn't anything serious or horrible, just colic, but it wasn't fun to hear her crying and to feel so helpless.

Dev didn't *do* helpless.

He'd sent his parents off to their vacation condo in Florida three weeks ago with a sigh of relief. Both the Brownes and the Palmers were acting way too protective of everyone involved, since his and Jodie's accident nine months ago. He often suspected that the Palmers would take DJ from him completely, if they could. Maybe he should take them up on that, relinquish custody and go back to New York.

But his heart rebelled at this idea, the way it often rebelled at the suffocating level of Palmer helpfulness. Jodie's mother and her two sisters here in Leighville seized on his need for babysitting too eagerly, he felt, trading on their combined experience of child-raising and his own helplessness. His parents had been taking a hand at it, too, but seemed suspicious that he was somehow being exploited, that Jodie had trapped him into this situation.

Which was ridiculous, since she didn't even know about it.

Today, despite his misgivings about the attitudes of both Palmers and Brownes, he could have done with some family help, but it wasn't possible, the way things stood. He was supposed to keep the baby safely away from the Palmer house.

Keep her away until Tuesday, the day after tomorrow, when Jodie had her appointment with doctors and therapists and counselors.

Zero hour.

His stomach kicked.

How did you prepare for something like that? He and the Palmers had been politely fighting about it for several weeks. The Palmers thought she still wasn't ready, while Dev couldn't handle the covering up, the distortions, the silence, even though he often dreaded what might happen once Jodie knew.

Doctor-patient ethics had become more of a concern with every step forward in Jodie's difficult recovery. There was an insistence now that she had the right to be told, and that she was strong enough, so the moment of revelation had been fixed for ten o'clock Tuesday morning.

What would she want? Where would he fit? Would she understand how much he loved this baby girl, this surprise package in both their lives? He felt an increasing need to know how it would all pan out—he hated uncertainty, and not knowing where he stood—but there was a lot to get through first. For a start, how did you say it?

Jodie, you need to know at this point that while you were in the coma state...

DJ wailed and shuddered in his ear, but maybe it was easing now. Was she too hot? Dev preferred open windows and the chance of a breeze to the shut-in feeling of an air-conditioned cocoon, but what would be best for the baby? He rocked her a little harder and she seemed to relax into his shoulder, her sweet, milky breath soft on his neck.

He loved her more than he'd imagined possible, and he had no idea what this was going to mean, once Jodie was told.

"Stop crying, sweetheart. That's right. Settle down, it's okay. Is your tummy still hurting? Not so much now, hey? Not so much..."

How did this happen to me?

Nine months ago he'd been enjoying a hot fling, ground rules fully in place, with a warm, funny and surprisingly gutsy woman, who'd turned his temporary return to Southern Ohio from an act of duty into an unexpected pleasure.

Thanks to Jodie, he'd stopped seeing a slow-paced backwater town and started seeing the beauty of the changing landscape in the fall. Instead of feeling the suffocation of routine, he'd felt the sinewy strength of family ties. He'd rediscovered the pleasure of a good laugh, of collecting the morning newspaper from the front yard while the grass was wet with dew, of hearing rain or birdsong outside his window instead of city noise.

But it was just an interlude. They both knew it. He'd said it to her direct, because he didn't want the risk of her getting hurt.

Even after the accident, he'd at first only planned to stay until his leg was put back together and healed. Jodie had family here. She wouldn't be on her own, whether she stayed in a coma state or made a full recovery. He didn't belong at her bedside, keeping vigil, the way her parents and sisters had.

But then...

DJ went through another spasm of pain and stiffened and screamed harder in his arms. "Ah, sweetheart, ah, honey-girl, it'll stop soon." He rocked her and massaged her little gut with the pad of his thumb.

How did this happen to me?

And what would change, come Tuesday?

Everything.

"Everything, baby girl," he murmured. Hell, he was so scared about it!

The knock at his front door startled him a few minutes later, the brass rapper hitting the plate unevenly, a couple of strong, jerky taps and then a weaker one. With DJ still in his arms, her crying beginning to settle to a kind of shuddery grumble, he went to see who was there, and when he saw Jodie standing there, he knew he didn't have until ten o'clock Tuesday anymore.

Zero hour was now.

The baby wasn't Lucy.

Jodie worked that out in around forty seconds, as she and Dev both stood frozen on either side of the threshold.

The baby wasn't Lucy, because Lucy belonged to Maddy and John, and had gone home with them to Cincinnati, and was smaller and newer than this little thing.

This little thing clearly belonged to Dev, and explained exactly why his crooning and shushing and swaying on Mom and Dad's back deck had been so effective earlier today. He'd had practice. Recent practice, and a lot of it.

"You'd better come in," he said heavily, after standing there in what appeared to be a frozen moment of shock. Jodie was pretty shocked herself. "I think she's going to sleep," he added. "You're not catching her at the best time. I wish you could see her smiling, the way she's been doing the past month "

"It's a girl?"

"Yes."

"What's her name?"

"I…uh…I call her DJ."

"DJ," she echoed blankly. He *called* her DJ. But it wasn't her name?

"You look like you need to sit. Shoot, of course you need to sit."

"Yes. I do." She hadn't realized it herself until now, despite her shaky hand on the heavy door knocker, but, yes, her legs had turned pretty shaky, too, and the frame wasn't giving enough support. She had no idea what was happening, here.

Dev had a baby.

He absolutely, one hundred percent *had...a...baby.*

He had a cloth thrown over his shoulder to catch the spit-up, and a hand cradling the baby's little diaper-padded butt as if it grew there, and a puffy rectangle of baby quilt in the middle of the floor, with a baby gym arched over it, like the one Maddy and John had brought to Mom and Dad's today for Lucy, even though their three-week-old infant could hardly be expected to play with such a thing.

This baby was definitely older. Dev had just mentioned she'd been smiling for the past month, and Jodie had enough nieces and nephews, thanks to all of Elin and Lisa's kids, that she knew when smiling happened—six weeks or so. This baby, small though she was, had to be getting on for about ten weeks old.

Do the math, Jodie, do the math. Nine months plus two and a half equals almost a year. When you were busy "getting the old crush out of your system," last fall, the mother of Dev's baby must already have been pregnant....

But where was the mother now? *Who* was the mother?

"Here. Sit here," Dev said, after she'd made her way inside. It was a pretty house, but the décor was too frilly and fussy for a man like Dev, with lace and florals and porcelain knickknacks everywhere. His mother's taste. "I'll take the frame. Do you want coffee, or something?"

"No. I— No, I'm fine."

"Look, it's obvious we need to talk. Let me get you something."

"Is—? Who else is around?"

"No one. My parents are in Florida. They have a condo there. I made them go."

"You *made* them?"

"Don't you sometimes feel…haven't you felt, these past few weeks, as if sometimes there's just too much family?"

"Ohh, yeah!"

That she could relate to.

But the baby…

DJ had fallen asleep on Dev's shoulder. "Hang on a sec," he muttered, and picked up a roomy piece of cloth that turned out to be a baby sling. He draped it across his shoulder, tucked the baby inside and stood there, still swaying gently. "If I put her down now, she'll just wake up again," he explained. "She needs to go a little deeper before it's safe."

"You're very good at it."

"Yeah…not really. I'm getting there. I have a who-o-ole heap of help."

A heavy silence fell, during which the obvious reference to DJ's mother wasn't made.

Dev said nothing about her.

Jodie didn't want to ask.

"She's adorable," she said instead, feeling woolly and wooden about it, wondering if she should be angry. Or hurt. Or just cheerful. *Wow, you have a baby, congratulations. You said you didn't want kids, but whoever the mom is obviously didn't get the memo.*

Unless of course…

Well, accidents happened. Baby-producing accidents, as well as ones that break legs in three places and put people into comas and necessitate the removal of spleens. Dev and some unknown woman had had a contraceptive "oops" roughly eleven months ago, and here was a baby, and her mom had probably just run to the store for diapers and milk. She and Jodie would meet each other any minute now.

"I can't take this in," she blurted.

"I don't blame you. Jodie, this was all set up for Tuesday. Does your family know you're here? They couldn't!"

"Oh, my family... Didn't you just ask me if I felt there was too much family? Well, there is! I said I was going for a walk and I didn't need company. I just told them around the block, and that if I wasn't back in forty-five minutes, send a search party. Coming here was an impulse."

"I'd better call your folks." He rocked the baby in his arms instinctively.

"It hasn't been forty-five minutes."

"You're going to be here for a while." He'd already picked up the phone and hit speed dial, as if the matter was urgent.

He has my parents on speed dial, she registered. But she liked his directness, the decisive way he moved. It was reassuring, somehow. Dependable.

He spoke a moment later. "Hi, Barb?" Barb was Mom. "Just letting you know, Jodie's here.... Nope, not my idea... No choice, at this point... I can't argue it now, you have to trust me.... Of course I will... No. Just me. Please... Yep, okay, talk soon."

"What was that about, Dev?" She tried to stand up, but her legs wouldn't cooperate. The walk had tired her more than she wanted.

"We've both said it. Too much family."

"Right."

"First, tell me why you came. I mean, what made you

think—? What gave you the idea—?" He broke off and swore beneath his breath. "Just tell me what made you come."

His difficulty in finding the right words made her flounder a little, and struggle for words herself. "I wanted to ask you...or to thank you, too, for coming to see me in the hospital those times."

"Just that?" He sounded cautious, looked watchful, as if waiting for a heck of a lot more.

"Well, and for—I don't know if I'm even the reason for this, or even *part* of the reason, but...not going back to New York when you planned."

"Hell, of course I wasn't going back to New York!"

She looked at him blankly and he understood something—something that *she* didn't understand at all, but she could see the dawn of realization in his face, while her body stopped belonging to her and belonged...somewhere else, to someone else.

It was a familiar feeling. Just the accident and her slow recovery? Or something more?

He was muttering under his breath. Curse words, some of them. And coaching. He was coaching himself. He sat down suddenly, in the armchair just across from the couch, with the sling-wrapped baby cradled in his arms, as if his legs had drained of their strength just like Jodie's had.

"*Pretend* I've just been in a coma for nearly nine months, Devlin," she said slowly. "Tell me anything you think I might not know. *Pretend* my family has a habit of shielding me from the most pointless things. And from the serious things, too. And tell me even the things you think I already do know. What did you mean, *set up for Tuesday?* What did you mean, *no choice at this point?* And this might be totally off-topic, but how is there a baby? And where is her mom?"

Chapter Three

She doesn't know. She doesn't understand.

The realization kept cycling through Dev's head, paralyzing him. Hell, he hadn't wanted it to happen like this! He'd been so scared of the moment, sometimes—scared about what it would mean for his own bond with his baby girl. What if Jodie wanted the baby all to herself? What if he was suddenly shut out? He wasn't prepared to let that happen, but how tough would he be willing to get about custody and access, when Jodie's recovery was still so far from complete? What would be best for DJ?

He'd wanted to get the revelation over with, so that at least he would begin to know where he and DJ stood, but the timing had to be right. It had to be done in the right way.

With all the talk, the questions, the arguments back and forth between pretty much every member of the

Browne and Palmer families for weeks, the conjectures that maybe at some level she knew, and that some tiny thing might easily jog a memory, no one had considered that Jodie herself might be the one to determine when they broke the news.

Devlin had wanted her told sooner, and his parents had been on his side. The Palmers had wanted to wait, insisting she wasn't ready for such a massive revelation. The doctors, therapists and counselors wanted to respect the family's wishes, but had been growing more insistent with each stage in Jodie's improvement, after the setback of the serious infection she'd had just after DJ was born.

This was part of the problem. It had all happened in stages. It wasn't as if she'd just opened her eyes one day and said, "I'm back. Catch me up on what I've missed!"

All through the coma there had been signs of lightening awareness, giving hope for an eventual return to consciousness, but it had been so gradual. First, she followed movement around the room with her eyes, but couldn't speak. It seemed so strange that she could have her eyes open without real awareness, but apparently this was quite common, the doctors said.

Then her level of consciousness changed from "coma" to "minimally conscious state." She began to vocalize vague sounds, but had no words. She started to use words but not sentences. She began to move, but with no strength or control. For several days she cried a lot, asking repeatedly, "Where am I? What happened to me?"

Once she'd understood and accepted the accident and the need for therapy, she'd become utterly determined to make a full recovery and had worked incredibly hard. Every day, over and over, in her hospital room, in the occupational therapy room, or the rehab gym, they all heard, "Don't bother me with talking now, I'm working!"

Barbara Palmer began to say, about the baby, "Not until she's home," and her therapists cautiously agreed that, emotionally, this might be the right way to go. Let her focus on one thing at a time. Don't risk setting back her physical recovery with such a shock of news.

How did you say it?

How the hell was he going to say it now?

You were five weeks pregnant at the time of the accident, it turns out, although we're almost certain you didn't know. You gave birth, a normal delivery, at thirty-three weeks of gestation, when your state was still defined as coma, just a week after you first opened your eyes. This is your beautiful, healthy baby girl.

He said it.

Somehow.

Not anywhere near as fluently as it sounded in his head.

"Sh-she's yours…Jodie," he finally said, stumbling over every word. Yours? No! He wasn't going to sabotage his own involvement. "She's *ours*," he corrected quickly. "I didn't know what to call her. I thought you'd want to decide. So she's been DJ till now, because those are our two initials. Is that okay? Are you okay? This was supposed to happen on Tuesday, at your appointment, with your doctors and therapists and people on hand to answer all your questions. To—to help you deal with it."

The words sounded stupid to his own ears. *Deal with it.* Doctors and counselors could help someone *deal with* a cancer diagnosis, but this was in a whole different league.

Her eyes were huge in her face. She couldn't speak. She was slightly built, which made a stark show of her current shock and vulnerability. He remembered thinking her funny and gawky and oddly impressive when she was sixteen and he was eighteen, and dating her friend. Impressive because she looked as if a breath of wind would blow her away, but, boy, did she get on your case if you treated her that way.

She'd been just the same in the hospital and during rehab, once she could speak and move. She'd insisted on her own strength and her own will, and proved with every step that she was as strong and determined as she claimed. She fought her family on it all the time, because she was seven years younger than her next sister and she'd had a serious brush with meningitis as a child, and the whole clan had babied her ever since.

Well, for once she wasn't fighting or insisting. She was too shocked. He'd half expected a protest or a denial. *You're messing with my head. It can't be true.* But she didn't say anything like that. She believed him at once, which made him wonder if there was a tiny, elusive part of her brain, or a lacing of chemicals— hormones—in her body that had known the truth.

Her conscious mind, though, and her sense of self, had been completely in the dark.

"I have a thousand questions," she blurted out.

"Of course. Ask them. I'll tell you everything as straight as I can."

"I can't."

"Ask them?"

"Do this." She tried to stand up, but her legs wouldn't carry her.

"Sit," he insisted. "You don't have to say anything. Or do anything. Let me talk, if you want."

"Okay."

So he talked, keeping it a little impersonal because that felt safe, and leaving out a few things, because he couldn't hit her with all of it at once.

He told her about the signs of labor, the quick delivery they'd all been praying for, to ease the stress on her body. Told her DJ's length and birth weight and head circumference. Told her proudly that the baby had Jodie's own strength. Despite her premature birth, DJ had been stepped down from the NICU into the lower-level special-care unit within a couple of days, and had come home from the hospital in less than two weeks.

"Home?" Jodie croaked.

"Here. And your parents' place. She spends a lot of time there." More than he was happy with, to be honest, but he hadn't wanted to fight them on that at a point when Jodie's full recovery had still been very much in doubt, and when his own future wasn't fully resolved. Would she ever be able to take care of a child? If she could, did that mean he'd go back to New York?

"Why are you here? In Leighville?"

She was asking the wrong questions, wasn't she? He took in a breath to suggest this to her, but then changed his mind.

Ah, hell, there was no script for this! She should ask whatever she wanted to, in whatever order it came. And if she didn't have an instant, overpowering need to hold DJ in her arms, he should be glad of the reprieve. He couldn't stand the idea of losing his daughter, not even with generous custody and access, when the bond between them had grown so strong.

"I'm still working at Dad's law practice," he explained, trying to stay practical and calm. "He's in no hurry to get back into harness. I expect he'll decide to retire. I'll head back to New York… Well, that's open-ended at the moment. All decisions on hold, I guess. My apartment is rented out. I have a conference coming up in Sweden in early October, followed by a couple of months consulting in London."

"You were supposed to be back in New York by last Christmas. Was it your dad's health that changed your plans?"

Shoot, didn't she understand?

"They found out you were pregnant before I even had the plates put in my leg."

"How?"

"Blood tests, part of assessing your condition. When they told me…" Again, how to say it?

"You knew you had no other choice," she supplied for him.

He couldn't argue. Not the words, anyway. Maybe the edge of—what?—bitterness, or anger, in her tone. He *hadn't* had any other choice. Not then. He wasn't going to abandon his child before it was even born. He wasn't going to deprive her of a father, when she might never have a mom. But it was different now. "I don't want another choice," he said. "This all needs time to work out, and that's okay."

"You said you didn't plan on ever having kids."

"You remember that?"

"Over dinner. You had steak with pepper sauce. I had strawberry mousse cake for dessert."

"Shoot, you do remember!"

"Yes. It's like yesterday, that mousse cake." The subtext of *explain yourself, Dev* was very clear. She wasn't really talking about dessert.

He said slowly, "What was it John Lennon once said?

'Life is what happens to you while you're busy making other plans.'"

"Or while you're in a coma," she drawled.

"Yeah, then, too."

Tentatively, they both smiled, and something kicked inside him. He had a couple of memories that were like yesterday to him, too. Her passion in bed, almost fierce, as if in lovemaking, too, she had to prove her own strength, had to fight against the wrong preconceptions. Her saucy grin when she undressed. And his ambivalence.

He really, seriously, hadn't known if it was a good idea to take her to bed that first time, even though she said she wanted it, and said she understood there was no long-term, and no promises, and that was fine. He'd told himself a couple of times their first night that he would stop kissing her soon, that he would reach out and still her hands if she went to pull off her clothes.

But then she'd done it. Crossed her arms over her chest and lifted her top to show a hot-pink bra and neat, tight breasts. Shimmied her way out of her skirt. Grinned at him.

And there'd been no question of stopping after that point. He'd used protection, but—not to get technical, or anything—maybe applied it just a little too late.

"But the dates don't fit," she said suddenly. "She's too old. She's smiling. Lucy isn't."

"Because DJ was premature," he explained again. "Healthy preemies learn to smile at the same age after birth as full-term babies, even if they're smaller and a little slower in other areas. DJ and Lucy would have been born within a week or two of each other, if DJ had come at the right time. The doctors say it's good that she didn't. It was easier on your body that she was little, and early. Would you like to hold her?"

He asked it before he thought. Blame Lucy for that. Jodie had looked so happy and comfortable holding her tiny niece today.

DJ was different. DJ had baggage.

Jodie stiffened and stammered. "No, she's—she's—N-not yet, when she's asleep. If I disturbed her and she cried…"

"It's fine. We'll transfer her in the sling. It'll be easy, I promise." Listen to him! Five minutes ago, he'd been scared about the strength of her maternal feelings and what they might do to his own connection with his child. Now he was trying to rush her into them. He didn't know what he wanted anymore.

Which was weird and unpleasant, because he *always* knew what he wanted.

Her weakened left hand made a claw shape on her thigh. "No. No, I can't. I just can't."

Jodie heard the note of panic in her own voice, but there was nothing she could do about it. The panic was there. She couldn't explain it to Dev. Couldn't even explain it to herself. But there was a huge, massive chasm of a difference between holding and clucking over Maddy's little Lucy and holding this baby.

My baby. Half an hour ago, I didn't know she existed. But she's mine.

It was overwhelming.

It should have been wonderful. A miracle.

Dev loves her. I can see it.

But it didn't feel wonderful, it felt terrifying.

Thank heaven Dev loves her, because I don't.

No. No! She had to love her own child! She did. Of course she did.

But why couldn't she feel it? Why wasn't it kicking in at once, the way it had with Elin and Lisa and Maddy and all the other normal mothers in the world, the very first moment they looked at their babies? Dev clearly expected it to, with his urging that DJ would be safe in her arms. It wasn't a question of safety. Why could she feel so tender toward Lucy today, and yet so distant and scared about this baby?

Scared? A surge of strength hit her. She wasn't in the habit of giving in to *scared*. She took in a breath to tell him that she would hold the baby after all. And she would have reached out her hands before the words came, except they were a little slow to respond to her brain's signal and she had to make an extra effort.

But before either the movement or the words could happen, Dev accepted her refusal, gave her an easy excuse. "You're tired," he said. He let out a breath that might have been partly relief, as if maybe he'd doubted the strength and coordination in her arms more than he'd let on. "We should wait a little."

She almost argued.

Almost.

But, oh, he was right, she was tired, and she'd tried so hard to stay on top of everything today. She let it go, and watched him tiptoe to the infant car carrier sitting in the corner of the living room and lay the baby down, easing his forearm out from beneath her little head with a movement so practiced and gentle it almost broke her heart.

"Very tired," she managed to respond. "I'm sorry."

I'm so sorry, DJ.

"Don't beat yourself up." The baby stirred a little, but didn't waken.

"I—I—" Did he know? Did he understand the extent of her panic?

"Let's take it slow. It's okay."

"Thanks. Yes."

She heard a car in the driveway, and footsteps and the voices of Elin and Mom. Dev lunged for the door before they could knock. He held it open and stood with the width of his body shielding the room from their view.

Mom said, "Is she still here?"

"Yes, but why are *you* here, Barb? I asked you very clearly to—"

"I'm sorry, we just couldn't— I'm sorry." This was Elin, clearly reading his anger. "We have a right to be involved in this, too, don't we? DJ is ours, too. We all care so much."

"You'd better come in."

"Thank you," said Mom, in a crisp voice.

"I really think it's best, Devlin." This was Elin, in a softer tone.

"We are as involved in all of this as you are." Mom again.

They dropped at once to sit on either side of Jodie on the couch, their voices running over her along with their hands, all of it a jumble that she heard at two steps removed, like recorded voices or lines from a half-remembered play. *Honey, are you okay? Obviously you know. Obviously there's so much to talk through. That's why we wanted to wait until you were ready. What has Dev said, so far?*

"You barely gave me time to say anything," he said.

"Listen, it's not as if any of us have had any experience with a situation like this, Devlin," Elin said.

"Shh…keep your voice down, can you?"

"Sorry...sorry." Elin glanced over at the baby and looked surprised. "You have her in the car carrier?"

"She seems to sleep better in there, during the day."

"Well, then, I guess..." *But I never did that with my babies,* was the implication.

"She's fine. She wouldn't sleep so peacefully if she was uncomfortable there."

"If you say so."

Both Devlin and Elin were holding it together with difficulty, and Mom looked trapped and unhappy, her mouth open as if she wanted to speak, although no words came.

Jodie slumped against the back of the couch. She'd started to shake. Could they feel it? She felt more tired than she'd ever felt in her life, and her lips had gone dry. She closed her eyes, willing this chaos of family and tension and questioning to...just...stop.

"Should we take her? Jodie, are you ready to go home?"

She opened her eyes. "Yes, take her."

I mean, who is she? How can she even exist?

"I—I don't know what I want to do," she blurted. "I think I need some space. Another nap." Her own bed seemed like the safest haven in the world.

There was a small silence, while Elin and Mom and Devlin all looked at each other, shrugged and raised eyebrows and gestured—body language that was beyond Jodie's ability to interpret right now.

"I guess that's an option," Dev said slowly to Elin and Mom. "For you to take her and Jodie to stay here."

"That's not—" *What I meant.* But the rest of it wouldn't come, and the first bit had come almost on a whisper, and they were too busy making plans to hear her.

"She should transfer to the car without waking," Dev said. "I have a couple of bottles made up in the fridge."

"We have bottles. We have diapers, clothes, everything. You know that. She's due for her bath."

"I'll drop Jodie home when she's ready. She's right. We need to talk. Have some space."

They'd worked it all out between the three of them, while Jodie was still struggling to lift an arm to brush a strand of damp hair from her eyes. She was staying here with Dev to talk. The baby was going back with Mom and Elin. Going back before she, the mother, had even touched her.

She wanted to argue the plan, but the words wouldn't come, so in the end she let it happen, and when the baby carrier was buckled into the car and Mom and Elin had driven away, she felt so relieved, and so ashamed of the relief, and so horribly, horribly tired. "I can't—" she said to Dev.

"I know you can't talk yet. Sleep first."

"Two naps a day. I'm like—" She stopped.

A baby.

My baby.

"Just rest."

"Why aren't you in New York? Tell me why. In simple words. Because it seems to me that you didn't have to still be here. Obviously DJ is being taken care of. Obviously she's loved. Obviously I have the support. So why?"

He looked at her steadily, with some of the anger he'd clearly felt toward Elin and Mom still simmering below the surface. He seemed to be thinking hard before he chose his words.

"Because she's my daughter." The last two words came out with a simmering intensity. "Because we're a family. You and me and DJ. Three of us. That's not negotiable. Three of us, not two."

"A family…" Jodie echoed foolishly, tasting the word and not feeling sure of how it felt in her mouth.

"Not a regular family, for sure."

"No…"

"But DJ needs a family of some kind.…" He paused for a moment, and she filled in the words he didn't say, in her head. *And not necessarily a whole cluster of over-involved grandparents and aunts.* "I'm right here in the picture and I'm not going to go away. And we have a heck of a lot to do and talk and think about, to decide how that's going to work."

Chapter Four

Jodie woke to the smell of something delicious coming from Dev's kitchen. The daylight had begun to fade, which meant she must have slept a good three hours this time. She felt disoriented and not in full possession of either her body or her brain. It was just the way she'd felt coming out of the coma. It was like being in the eye of a hurricane—eerily quiet, with a sense of danger all around.

She gave herself a couple of minutes to regroup, then sat up and eventually stood, steadier on her feet than she would have expected. As before, Dev had left her walking frame within reach, and the quiet, considerate nature of this small gesture almost brought her to tears.

She could hear him in the kitchen, chopping something on a wooden board. The delicious aroma announced itself as beef sizzled in a pan. She'd had a crush on him thirteen years ago, she'd slept with him three times, and she'd had no idea until now that he could cook. It didn't surprise her, though. When Devlin Browne put his mind to something...

He heard her—the rubbery tap of the frame on the floor—as she reached the kitchen doorway, and he turned. "Hi. Better?"

"Think so. It's crazy. To need all that sleep."

"Your brain is still healing."

"So I've been told."

"I'm making brain food. A beef-and-vegetable stir-fry, full of iron and vitamins."

"It smells great."

"Ready in a couple of minutes. Sit down." He nodded at the wooden kitchen table, then moved to pull out a chair for her.

"No, don't," she said quickly, taking one hand off the frame to reach for the chair herself. "I'm fine. I hate—" *my family hovering over me* "—too much help."

"Duly noted." He turned back to the stove, tossed in slivers of onion and red bell pepper, sticks of carrot and celery, lengths of green bean. The pan hissed and made a cloud of aromatic steam, filling the silence made by their lack of conversation.

He seemed to understand instinctively that she didn't want to talk yet—or not about anything important, anyway—and to her surprise the interlude of silence between them felt easy and right. She didn't have that uncomfortable itch to break the quiet with a rush of words that people often experience in the company of someone new.

Not that Dev was new.

But this felt new.

Untested.

Three of us. We're a family, he'd said.

Anything but the usual kind.

She watched him. Just couldn't help it. The way his neat, jeans-clad butt moved as he tossed the contents of the pan. The way his elbow stuck out and his shoulder lifted. He added the cooked meat and leaned back a little as another cloud of hissing steam came up. There was rice in a steamer on the countertop, and a jug of orange juice clinking with a thick layer of cubed ice.

Nine months ago, he hadn't wanted a serious relationship, but now it was as if she'd simply blinked and woken up to find herself here, in his kitchen, and the mother of his child.

Connected.

Yet not.

Are we dating?

She felt they needed to talk about it—for *hours* surely—but had no idea what to say, what to suggest. He was the one who'd had time to think. The surge of chemistry she'd felt earlier at the family barbecue couldn't compete with her shock and disorientation. It hummed in the background of her awareness, but she didn't know what to do with it, just wished it would go away.

"Is there a schedule?" she blurted out.

"A schedule?"

"Of who takes care of—of DJ."

DJ. That's my baby's name. Well, it's not her name. It's what we're calling her in the interim.

A crazy litany of baby names began to scroll in her head, the ones she'd vaguely thought, over the years, that she liked. Caroline, Amanda, Genevieve, Laura, Jessica, Megan, Anna… The idea that it might be up to her to make a decision, replace temporary DJ with something different and permanent that would belong to the baby her whole life, was daunting. A huge, confusing responsibility that she didn't feel equipped to handle.

"Your family has her when I'm at work," Devlin answered. "Mainly your mom. She's set up Elin's room for a nursery."

"That's why Lucy had to sleep in my room today." An image flashed in her head of her sister's old room with the door firmly closed. Even if she had seen inside, she would have assumed it had been set up for Maddy's baby girl.

"But Elin and Lisa have her sometimes, too. And then I pick her up on my way home."

"The night shift."

"That's right. I expect she'll spend more nights at your parents' place now." *Now that you're home,* he meant.

"That's why you look tired." A rush of tenderness and guilt ran through her. Those creases around his eyes, and she hadn't been here to help. Crazy to feel that it was her fault, and yet at some level she did. What kind of a mother slept through her whole pregnancy and didn't even waken to give birth? What kind of a mother had an eleven-week-old baby that she'd never touched and held?

He made a wry face. "Yeah, she's not exactly sleeping through. Your sisters have been great with that. They've stayed over here three or four times to give me a good night. Your whole family has been—" He stopped, as if the word he'd originally intended to say was wrong. "Amazing. They have. I was a little short with them before, and I shouldn't have been. The boundaries—the roles—are complicated."

"It's okay. I know how you feel. Just be thankful they're not trying to cut up your food."

He laughed and she smiled at him and then her breath caught, and the question she'd been asking in her head even before she'd found out about DJ came blurting out, "Are we dating, Dev?"

He went still. She just knew he was going to say no. It was there in his body language so clearly, and she wondered why on earth she'd thought it necessary to ask. Well. She hadn't thought. Her brain didn't seem to control either her body or her words anymore.

Eventually answered in a slow, careful way, "That's a question, isn't it?"

"I mean, I'm not suggesting you have a thing for unconscious women." The humor didn't work. It was too dark for a moment like this. It didn't evaporate the tension, as intended. She apologized. Seemed as if she might be doing a lot of that. "I'm sorry. I was just—"

"It's okay. Lightening the mood. You had a right to ask. I talked about making a family, just now."

"When you came to see me in the hospital, I didn't know why you were there. Because I didn't know about DJ. And last fall we…"

"I know." He was still so uncomfortable. They both were.

"I don't think we're dating," she said, before he could say it. "It would be crazy. It's not what we need. It would just be a complication. We have enough of those."

He nodded, and looked relieved. "You're right. I guess that's what I've felt. First things first. Take care of DJ. Take care of you. Take all of it slow. You're not strong enough to do much with a baby right now. We want to find a way to share her and love her. There's no hostility or conflict. I want to keep it that way. We *have* to keep It that way. I want as much involvement as I can have."

"But she'll be with me most of the time." Was it a question, or a statement? She didn't even know.

"Once you know her," he said "Once you can take care of her. You're her mother and most of the time the baby stays with the mom. I'm accepting that."

But am I?

She saw herself stranded with baby DJ in her parents' house for weeks at a stretch with barely a break. She imagined the winter days closing in, keeping her and the baby inside the house, when normally even in the cold weather she loved to be outdoors.

These weren't the pictures she wanted to have of herself and her baby, but they were the ones that came. She heard herself wrangling and bickering with Mom about when to introduce solid food and whether to dress her in pink.

Dress her in pink...

She tried to picture it, and couldn't. At all. With a stab of horror she realized, *I don't remember what she looks like.* All she had were two vague images of a little face distorted with crying and then peaceful in sleep. Would she recognize her, beyond the familiarity of Dev's arms, or Mom's? Could she pull her own daughter out of a lineup?

Another bizarre image came to her. Police station. One-way glass. "Now, Ms, Palmer, look carefully at the numbered cribs. Do you see your baby here? It's very important that you make a correct identification."

But she couldn't...

"Dinner's up," Dev said. "I think we're— I'm glad we said this."

She tried to stand, to go over to the bench and help

him dish out the food, but her feet caught and she almost fell. He was there just in time.

"He-e-ey. Who-o-oa." He caught her and folded his arms around her. "You didn't have to get up. I'm bringing it to you."

She felt his breath fanning her hair and his chin resting on her shoulder, and could have stayed like this forever. She loved the way they fit together despite their mismatched size. She loved the smell of him, the strength of him, the honor and humor and decisiveness and brains. She loved the fact that he could hug her like this so soon after they'd agreed—the only thing they *could* agree on, in this situation—that they weren't dating anymore.

It was just a hug, and yet if she just turned her face up, she was sure he would kiss her. The chemistry was still there, a deep pool of it, secret and still, magical and unspoken.

She wanted him to kiss her.

Desperately.

Just kiss me, Dev, so I don't have to think. Just kiss me, so I know that part is okay, even if everything else isn't.

I don't care what we decided.

I don't care about sensible.

Kiss me and say, "Let's get married, and I'll take care of whatever you need," so that we can play by the rules and be a normal mommy and daddy and then maybe I'll feel as if I belong in my own life, instead of being just a visitor.

"This is the most insane situation," he muttered. "I don't know what to tell you. Just take your time. That's all. We all need to give this time."

Kiss me. Say it.

Shoot!

This neediness, this wasn't *her! Jodie Palmer, don't you remember who you are? You've been fighting your whole life to show how strong you are, and now you're clinging to Dev as if he has all the answers and so you can just go with the flow?*

The familiar stubbornness kicked in. Maybe a little off-center, but at least it was there, and the feeling came as a huge relief. She pulled out of his arms and crisply said, "Thanks. You're right. We'll give it time. We'll work it out. Thank you. Mmm, that smells good!"

He steered her the few steps back to her seat then turned toward the stove, blinking as if he'd opened his eyes in bright light, and she was so happy that she'd held herself together. What if she had clung to him and expressed all that neediness?

He spooned rice into wide bowls and added a ladle of the hearty stir-fry, then placed the bowls on the table, and as they began to eat—it tasted so good!—she found something she wanted to ask him that didn't have the sense of dependency and need she so wanted to fight in herself. "The other driver, Dev. I—I haven't felt ready to ask until now. And you know my family wouldn't bring it up without direct questions."

"No, they wouldn't. We've had a couple of discussions about that, too."

"I bet you have!" She folded her mouth into an upside-down smile. "Who was it? Were they injured, too? He? She?"

"He."

"What happened?"

Dev put down his fork. "He wasn't badly hurt. You don't need to know anything about him."

"You don't sound too sympathetic. What went wrong?"

"He was driving over the limit."

"Speed or alcohol?"

"Both."

"Ah, okay. All bases covered, then. A fine upstanding citizen." She gave another twisted smile.

He shrugged and opened his palms. "Exactly."

"And where is he now?"

"Tried and convicted. All you need to know."

"It happened and it's over, and now we just live our lives. That's it, isn't it?"

"Is that what you really think?"

She paused with the fork halfway to her mouth. Most of the food fell off. She was still a little wobbly with her silverware control. "Yes. Don't you?"

"Yes, I do. I was a little concerned that you might feel differently."

"That I'd want a vendetta? Or that I'd brood and feel bitter?"

"Many people would." He was leaning toward her over the table, studying her the way he'd studied her several times today. She knew why. How was this going to work? How would baby DJ connect or divide them? What did they both want? Could they manage to keep this free of conflict and misunderstanding and hurt? Everything came back to that. Everything they said to each other gave a potential clue.

"Well, not me," she told him. "I just like to get back on the horse."

"Mmm," was all he said.

But she could see something in his face. Relief and approval. It was something they shared, this attitude to the accident and how to process it, and that was a plus.

In life, you have to play the hand you're dealt. She believed this, and so did he. You can't waste energy in "if only" and regret. You can't go looking for bitterness and revenge.

Especially when she had other things to think about. Like a baby she didn't know she'd had.

Like a baby she wouldn't recognize in the street.

Too hard. Way too hard.

She felt a surge of restlessness and fight, a need for the physical movement that was still so challenging, and told him suddenly, "I seriously do want to get back on the horse."

"The real horse?" She'd caught his attention again. "You want to ride your horse again?" They were both making slow progress with their meal. "Your thoroughbred? He's leased out, since the accident, isn't he?"

"Leased out, to another rider, Bec, who's a good friend and who would give him back in a heartbeat. She lives out near Pictonville, on forty acres. I could go see him anytime. He's not sold."

She'd been so happy to discover this. Elin had told her, "Even though Mom's never been a fan of your riding, even in the darkest hours when we questioned how much you'd recover, she wouldn't hear of Irish being sold."

But now Dev said, "A spirited thoroughbred, Jodie? Twelve hundred pounds of muscle with a back higher than your shoulder?"

"Of course not yet," she said quickly. "Not him. I'd ride Snowy or Bess."

"Who are they? Are they quieter?"

"They're our hippotherapy horses, at Oakbank. They're trained for people like me, disabled riders and riders with special needs. You wouldn't believe how patient and understanding they are. They seem to know exactly what a rider is capable of, whether they have cerebral palsy or a missing limb or autism. I want to ride again. I need to ride. My life just can't change that much." She had to blink back tears, and was shocked at the way her emotions had shifted so fast. "Dev, I know this isn't what we should be talking about. We should be talking about...about DJ, but that's too big for me right now."

He reached across the table and covered her hand with his. "Nobody said we had to work everything out in one night."

"No. Okay. Good."

"Just eat. Talk about horses, if you want."

"I think I should go home after we eat."

"So I'll take you home."

"Thank you." She was tired of saying the words, but it seemed as if there were a thousand thank-yous she needed to give, and at least half of them belonged to Dev.

Jodie was quiet in the car, and Dev didn't push. It had been a huge day, for both of them.

Certain things stood out from the mess of conflicting emotions. First, the fact that she had never been given a real chance to hold DJ. He didn't know if that was his fault, if he should have made space for it—*forced* it—in the highly charged atmosphere between himself, Elin and Barb. Second, her wobbly little question about whether they were dating. Last fall seemed so long ago to him, but to her it must be so much fresher.

Those nights together. They were vivid and real for him if he thought about them, but too much had been overlaid since, and he didn't think about them often. He hadn't been in love with her last fall, and he couldn't have fallen in love with her during her long sleep. This wasn't Sleeping Beauty or Snow White.

There'd been desire in their relationship, yes…a ton of it. Care, even. But "in love" meant forever, and he couldn't see it, he wasn't open to it, not with anyone. It didn't fit with the way he saw himself and his life, and it never had.

He loved his parents. He admired them. They were good people. But marriage had made them so slow and staid. They never left their comfort zone. They never seemed to want newness or adventure or zest. His mother said it to him sometimes, with a combination of smugness and resignation. "You'll feel differently when you're married.… You won't care about those things when you're married with a family."

He'd seen it with most of his married friends, too. They began eating at the same restaurant every week. "They do such a good veal parmigiano." They didn't renew their passport when it expired. "We won't really travel until the kids are in college. Well, Orlando, of course, for the theme parks."

If marriage meant losing the capacity for curiosity and courage and adventure, he didn't want it. He'd decided this at twenty and nothing had yet happened to make him change his mind.

Not even DJ, because how would it be good for her, to submit to an institution he didn't want to belong to, purely for her sake?

All he wanted was to know that she was loved, so he could get his own life back on track and stop existing in this limbo of uncertainty.

He wondered what would be happening at the Palmer house. When he pulled into the driveway there was no visible light in DJ's room. The night-light would be too dim to show from the street. Was she down for the night? Should he take her home?

Jodie hadn't even touched her yet. Had he been wrong to let Barb and Elin whisk the baby back here? Should he have just ordered them to leave? He didn't want the conflict that came with their differing interpretations of what Jodie needed. He wanted to see the bond between Jodie and DJ, but he was scared of it, too.

Scared of its potential power.

He jumped out of the car and came around to open her door and help her out. For a moment, she looked as if she might protest, but she was clearly too tired to manage on her own. The doctors and therapists had said it would be like this. The difference between what she could manage when she was fresh and what she could manage when she was fatigued might be huge at first.

Sure enough, her body looked heartbreakingly awkward and frail in the passenger seat, and after several seconds of intense, futile effort, she told him, "I can't."

He bent down. Slid his arm beneath hers and around her shoulders. "Hold on."

But she couldn't do that, either.

"I'll carry you."

"Dev, no, I'm—"

"You're wiped."

He shifted position, one arm coming beneath her thighs. It was incredibly awkward, and if she hadn't been such a featherweight, he couldn't have managed it. Once he'd straightened, it was much easier. She laid her head against his shoulder, with her hip pressing into his stomach, and he felt this surge of tenderness and confusion and determination.

Somehow... *Somehow...*

Somehow, what?

What did he have the power to do? To make her get better? To make her come to the right decisions about her future? What were they?

"You can put me down now."

"I'm fine. You don't weigh much."

"Please." There was an insistence to it, the old stubbornness about her size and strength that had made him smile and piqued his interest at eighteen. How did such a small body house such a strong spirit?

Gently, he let her down, still holding her firmly until they both knew that her feet would carry her weight. They did, but there wasn't a whole lot of margin for error. "I'll need to lean," she said.

"Leaning is fine." Leaning was *too* fine, really. He liked touching her too much, felt too connected to the scent and softness of her skin. He had to fight to keep his awareness under control, with the slight weight of her breasts just above his hand and her silky fall of blond hair in kissing distance.

They'd agreed on this. They weren't dating. There was no place for this helpless attraction. Just imagine if they had a flaming purely-for-the-sex affair and then parted in conflict and anger. It happened all too often. Sex didn't solve anything. It had too much of an agenda of its own.

And where would that leave him? Shut out of DJ's life forever? Or limited to a hard-won weekend visit every three months, exchanging her back and forth in the parking lot of a service-plaza fast-food restaurant halfway between here and New York as if she were a packet of cocaine? Meeting her at the airport, once she was old enough, and discovering she'd become a school kid or an adolescent or an adult since they'd last met?

No. It wouldn't be enough. No!

He wasn't going to be forced back to New York by the sheer strength of Palmer will.

Barbara Palmer stood in the open doorway, having heard the car. She looked watchful and anxious, as if expecting them to have covered major mileage tonight in their talks about the future.

They hadn't.

They'd barely talked about DJ at all. More about horses, in fact. And no matter how much Dev told himself to go with what Jodie needed, to give her time and space, it worried him a little. He didn't want to lose his daughter to her mother, but he wanted her mother to love her. Anything else was unthinkable.

"Did you have a good evening, honey?" Barb said to Jodie.

She thumbed cheekily in his direction. "I never knew he could cook."

"Are you okay? You look—"

"Tired. Of course. But I'm fine." She managed the steps into the house. In some ways she was better on steps than on the flat ground. "I think I'll go up right away."

"She's asleep," Barb said.

But Jodie hadn't been talking about seeing DJ. From the side, Dev saw the little look of fright and reluctance on her face and said quickly, "We'll take a look at her, though, Barb." He still had his arm around Jodie's body and could feel her stiffen and flinch.

Barb had seen nothing, it seemed. She began, "You're not going to—?"

"No, I'll leave her here for the night," he reassured her, "if that's okay."

"Of course it is! Of course you shouldn't wake her and move her!"

"But we'll take a look, make sure she hasn't kicked off her covers." He pretended he couldn't tell that Jodie didn't want to.

Why didn't she?

Well, the hugeness of it. It made sense, maybe. She just needed that first bit of ice broken, that first sense of confidence in her new role, that was all. Maybe right now, if they just went into the baby's room together and watched her sleeping, something in her heart would open and settle.

He didn't give her a choice, just took her with him, helping her up the stairs, opening the door of Elin's old room, which was as familiar to him now as if it had once been his. Beside him, he heard Jodie's quick, shaky intake of breath, as if Elin's door was the gateway to a whole new kingdom.

Chapter Five

Mom had used Elin's room as a sewing den for years but hadn't redecorated since Elin moved out. In Jodie's memory, the walls were still painted a defiant, brooding purple and were covered in posters of Elin's teen heartthrobs—John Cusack, Michael J. Fox and Johnny Depp. Actually, Elin in her teens had had pretty good taste.

Now, though...

There was a ballerina night-light plugged into the socket low on the wall beside the crib, Jodie saw. It gave off a quiet, pinkish light, revealing a room utterly different to the one she'd always known. Gone were the purple and posters, to be replaced by walls of a soft golden yellow with a theme of ducks and daisies in the scattered groupings of toys and decorations. There was a crib made of blond wood, with linens of white *broderie anglaise* cotton, a white closet, chest of drawers and shelves, and in just a couple of places there were color accents in a light sage-green.

On the chest of drawers sat the baby monitor, its glowing light showing that it was switched on. But there was nothing to hear. Baby DJ was fast asleep

Dev went across to her as if drawn like a magnet, his feet incredibly soft on the polished hardwood floor, a grin breaking onto his face in a way that told Jodie he didn't even know it was there. He had Jodie's hand trapped—not trapped, *held*—in his, so she had no choice but to go with him. He leaned over the crib and didn't say a word, just gazed, and Jodie's heart began to thump and her throat tightened, and the baby...the baby...

Didn't belong to her.

Was gorgeous, an angel, a sweetheart, a darling.

A stranger, when she should have been Jodie's whole world.

She knew this, because she'd seen it just today with Maddy and Lucy. Beyond the new-mother panic, or as a *part* of the new-mother panic, Maddy had been utterly mesmerized by Lucy, utterly in love with her. The way Elin had been with her firstborn, and her second and third. The way Lisa had been with hers.

Transformed.

Mothers to their bones.

The way Dev was already a father to his bones. A daddy. DJ's daddy. "Isn't she beautiful?" he whispered, as if he couldn't keep back the words.

"Yes. Yes, she is." She learned the baby's little face off by heart —the button of a nose, the plump cheeks— and thought, *at least I'll recognize her now...*

"I'm sure she won't wake up if you touch her."

"How? Where? I mean, I really don't want to wake her up."

"You won't. Anywhere."

Where would I touch her if she belonged to me?

Jodie didn't know. She reached out her hand, and felt Dev holding her tight as if he knew she might otherwise fall. She thought she might put her hand on DJ's head, to see if her hair felt as silky as Lucy's, but it didn't feel right. It felt...

Not her head.

She laid her palm on the baby's back, instead. She was sleeping on her side, propped in that position with two little baby quilts rolled up, so Jodie had to slip her fingers between the roll and the stretchy fabric of DJ's miniature pink sleep suit.

"She's breathing, I promise," Dev said.

"Oh, I wasn't— I was just—"

"It's okay. I didn't mean— It's okay. I check that she's breathing all the time."

But she didn't feel as if it was okay, and took her hand away. She wasn't strong enough to keep her arm in that position for long anyhow. It would start to disobey the signal from her brain pretty soon and just flop.

Flop onto DJ and wake her up.

Mom was hovering outside, peering around the door, which Dev had left ajar. "I thought about putting the monitor in your room, honey, but that's probably not a good idea just yet," she said in a kind of stage whisper as Jodie and Dev came out. "It would be hard for you to get out of bed quick enough to go to her."

Would I need to go to her that fast? Jodie wondered. Do all normal moms leap out of bed the second they hear the first tiny cry? What about in the dark, ancient days before baby monitors were invented? How fast did moms get to their babies back then?

She could argue the issue. She could insist on Mom letting her have the monitor.

Dev had gone watchful again, but she hid her panic, made it about common sense instead. "Yes, you'd better have it, Mom. I'd hate to…you know…" She indicated the common-sense issues with a flap of her fingers.

I'd hate to only reach her after that big spotty monster hiding under her crib had already drooled all over her. I'd hate no one to get there in time to catch her reciting Shakespeare in her sleep.

"I know. I think you're right. I'm sure that's the best decision," Mom said, as if it were momentous, like deciding on risky corrective surgery, or what college DJ would attend. "We can keep it that way as long as you want. Well, when she's sleeping here, of course."

Dev said nothing.

"I've done a spreadsheet," Barb announced when Dev arrived back at the Palmers' house the next morning.

"A spreadsheet?"

"I can do one every week. Here's a copy I printed out for you. The schedule has gotten more complicated now that Jodie is home, but see the color coding?"

Dev took the page. Yes, indeedy, he could see the color coding. Yellow for Jodie's hours at day rehab, blue for DJ's naps, even though she wasn't nearly as predictable in that department as the spreadsheet suggested. Green apparently meant DJ at Devlin's and he didn't like the scattered nature of those color blocks. So he was only having her two nights this week? Whose idea was that?

Barb had said to him some weeks ago, when Jodie's recovery began to unfold with such positive signs, "Now you'll be able to go back to New York," and he couldn't get those words out of his head. Did the Palmers want him to go? Did he?

Meanwhile, where was pink for Dev, Jodie and DJ go to the park? Or, better, lilac for Barb, Elin and Lisa get the hell out of town for a few hours so Jodie can make up her own mind about what she wants to do with the baby?

In fact, he couldn't see one color block or notation in the schedule that gave Jodie any time with DJ on her own.

"I mean, it's just a draft, obviously," Barb said, reading the disapproval in his face.

He said in apology, "I'm not a huge fan of spreadsheets, to be honest."

"But you must use them all the time, in your work."

"People put them together on my behalf. And I file them in the cylindrical file." He mimed balling a sheet of paper and tossing it in the trash.

"You throw them *out?*"

"Spreadsheets can make you feel like you're organized when really you're not, don't you think? Like bullet-point presentations. I'm not a fan of bullet points, either." He dropped the flippant tone and spoke gently, because despite everything, he was becoming fond of his daughter's grandmother. He knew she meant well. "You know DJ won't nap to a schedule, Barb, so why pretend about it on paper? We don't know how much time Jodie's going to be spending with her at this stage. Can't we keep it flexible?"

Barbara pressed her fingertips to her temples. "I'm just trying to manage this situation."

"I know. And I appreciate it. But I don't think a spreadsheet is the answer. Where are they, anyhow?"

"DJ is in her bassinet on the deck. I just gave her a bottle. Elin was helping Jodie in the shower, but I think they're done."

"So Jodie's upstairs?"

"Let me call her. I'm sure she hasn't come down."

He hesitated. It bothered him that Jodie wasn't with the baby, and yet why should it? What did he expect? He'd been so afraid of the opposite happening, of the love kicking in too fiercely and possessively and shutting him out, and now he'd done a full turn-around and wanted to push the other way.

It wasn't logical. *He* wasn't logical. He was a mess of conflicting wants—to go back to his real career in international law, yet keep the strongest possible bond with DJ, to see Jodie discover her love, yet for that love to be generous when it came to his own needs.

Jodie had huge needs of her own. She still struggled to manage dressing and showering and the most ordinary day-to-day things. She was so brave about it. Brave and funny and stubborn. She couldn't have taken over all of DJ's care even if she wanted to.

Did she want to? This was the crunch, the big question. Was she holding back from DJ in order to work harder on her own recovery, or because she couldn't cope with suddenly being a mom?

"I'll go up," he told Barb.

"I'll be in the kitchen, if you need me," she said. "You'll…say the right things, won't you?" Her face twisted with worry and he felt his frustration build. What did Barb want from him? It would help so much if she could just relax a little.

He found Jodie in her room doing some range-of-motion exercises for her arms and legs. She wore calf-length black leggings and a strappy white tank, little more than a scrap of stretch fabric and lace. The swell of her breasts peeked above the neckline of the tank, and the leggings made her tight, round butt seem even tighter and rounder. Dev had trouble keeping his gaze where it belonged.

But there was a serious point to the stretchy clothing. She was working hard. There was a sheen of sweat across her forehead and her collarbone, and she lifted her top away from her stomach to let in some air. "Nothing's working this morning," she said, slightly breathless. "Starting to come back a little."

"How about doing them on the deck?" He didn't like the way she was shut in her room like this, with DJ out of sight and out of mind.

"I guess that would be okay."

She managed the stairs on her own, while he went a few steps ahead of her, ready to brace her if she fell. When they reached the deck and she saw the bassinet with its lacy white canopy, she froze for a moment. She hadn't known until now that DJ was out here. "Oh, right," she murmured, then began to grab the air with her hand as if seeking something solid for support. Dev helped her get comfortable on the built-in wooden bench that ran along the railing and went to peek at his daughter.

She'd woken up. The wicker of the bassinet creaked a little as she tensed her body and let out a whimpering cry. She writhed, as if her digestion was bothering her, but then her gut settled and she blinked a few times and looked up at the view. Dappled leaves. Dev had learned that small babies, when awake, just lo-o-ove to look at dappled leaves with a background of sky.

Ooh, and here's something else they love to look at—their daddy. She caught sight of him and her face broke into the darlingest smile in the world. "That's right, sweetheart," he whispered, and smiled back. He was pitifully in love with her, and "in love" meant forever, and he didn't even care.

Jodie was watching him, he could see, distracted from the exercises she'd been so dedicated about up in her room. He felt a thud of sudden vulnerability—all that fear of the unknown where DJ's future was concerned.

He had to bite the bullet.

They both did.

Jodie had to have her first hold.

He didn't give her a choice today, just picked DJ up—she was wearing a stretch-cotton smock dress with tiny blue flowers on a white background, and matching bloomers—and brought her across. "Here, why don't you take her for a bit?"

"I—I— Now?" Jodie stammered.

"Yes, but you need a couple of cushions, right?"

"I think so."

"I'll grab some." He was more than capable of managing a baby and two cushions at once. He'd recently managed a baby, a poopy diaper and a handful of wipes with a phone pressed to his ear at the same time, talking international law. He settled the cushions on either side of her.

"Can you...? I'm leaning, I think."

She was right. Her body had slipped a little on the bench. He sat down beside her and nudged her bare, pale shoulder with his.

"I hate this," she said.

"*Hate* it?"

"No… No!" she corrected quickly. "Not the baby! Not her. My body. The fact that sometimes I'm not co-ordinated enough to sit straight, by myself."

"Right. You'll get there."

"I know. But it's frustrating." She sounded wobbly. Scared. Maybe she didn't hate the idea of holding the baby, but she definitely had issues with it. Because she didn't trust her body?

"I would never let her fall," he said, and lifted the baby across.

This is my baby. To Jodie it still didn't seem real. *This is my baby, in my arms.*

DJ didn't seem to consider this event to be miracu-lous in any way. She looked up at Jodie, fixing her gaze just below her hairline. She didn't smile. Her eyes were a dark, swimmy blue and she had translucent blisters on her lips from sucking on her bottle. The neckline of her tiny dress was still a little damp from where some of the formula had leaked from the corners of her mouth. She felt heavy.

No, it wasn't the weight, it was the tension in Jodie's muscles. "I didn't feel this tired, holding Lucy yester-day," she said.

Dev had risen and moved away. He stood on the far side of the deck, beneath the thickest shade from the black-cherry tree, watching her to check that she was all right. "You were in a chair with armrests for that," he said. "And Lucy's a little lighter than DJ. Can you not manage it? Let me know if—"

"No, I want to." Something kicked inside her, a stir-ring of tenderness and love. But it wasn't strong enough. It wasn't the overwhelming certainty Jodie wanted it to be.

I love her, she said inside her head.

No, that wasn't quite right.

She tried again. *I love you!*

It was true. She knew it was. But she couldn't *feel* it. She looked down at the baby, smiled at her and learned by heart every crease in her little arms, every strand of her hair, but she couldn't *feel* her love.

Those swimmy blue eyes looked up at her, so serious and unsmiling and somehow so wise and *old*.

She'll see it. She'll feel it. She'll know.

She still wasn't smiling. Jodie tried to coax it out of her by showing her how. She stretched her lips, crinkled her eyes. *This is your mommy smiling at you, DJ.* But it didn't work. DJ didn't smile back, and Jodie knew why.

You couldn't tell lies with your own body. You couldn't fake love coming out of every pore of your skin. Lying here in her arms, DJ would soon know that this person, this mommy person who was supposed to have such a total skin-to-skin bond and connection, didn't yet love her in the right way, and she absolutely *must not* be allowed to know that.

Jodie broke into a sweat. "Can you take her, Dev?"

"Or I could give your arm some more support."

"No, take her. I don't think more support would be enough."

"Here…" he said, and sat down beside her again, twisting around so that his left arm cradled hers and his chest shored up her shoulder. His strength and warmth and clean male smell slammed into her, seeming far more *right* than the feel of a baby in her arms. More real. Stronger. Could he feel it, too? She thought so. His breathing had changed, growing shallower.

She felt weak and shaky and tingling with need, all at the same time. Her body was far better at remembering familiar things than learning new ones, it seemed. Every cell and all her senses remembered last year so vividly. The way his touch and his laughter had set her alight, the way she'd felt strong and alive yet safe in his arms. The feel of his mouth making a hot trail from her neck to her breasts. The sureness in the way he caressed her, slipping his hand between her thighs, curving his palms over her butt.

Last year, he would have pressed his lips to her neck and teased her and set her on fire. She would have turned her face toward him and kissed him back, brushing her mouth against his and sliding it away, making him go after her and coax her lips into parting and drinking him in, and it would have lasted for minutes on end. She would have gloried in the feel of those hard muscles covered in satiny skin.

Their physical connection was magic and wonderful and made her dizzy.

Still.

But the new thing, the magic and wonder and dizziness of being a mother, her body couldn't learn. She couldn't even *fake* a smile now. No wonder DJ wasn't smiling back.

"I really think you need to take her now, Dev," she said shakily.

Mom appeared in the doorway to the deck. She was wearing a flour-spattered apron, and was brushing her hands against it, as if dusting them off in readiness to be of help. She must have heard the note of panic in Jodie's voice, the panic that Dev had ignored.

"No, see?" he said quietly. "You're fine."

"I—I think I'm not. I think I need a break. Can you please take her?"

He still wouldn't. Instead, he pressed his body more

tightly against her, curved his other arm over her shoulder to support her on the opposite side. Her back wasn't touching the bench at all now, it was only touching him, and she began to take calming breaths, giving in to his insistence and certainty.

Maybe she could do it, after all. Maybe with him here, loving his baby girl so much, the love would filter into Jodie as well, filter through her into DJ so that wise DJ wouldn't guess who it really came from. She could smell the mingled scents of both of them, Dev and DJ. Baby powder and milkiness and aftershave and warm male skin.

Mom stepped forward. "Dev, she says she's tired. Don't push it, please, until after we've talked to her doctors and therapists on Tuesday."

"Does that make a difference?" He slid his hand around the bundle of baby.

"Well, yes, doesn't it? They may have very specific guidelines about how much she's allowed to do."

"How much baby holding?"

"How much child care. How much of anything. She has a heap of exercises to get through every day. Just brushing her teeth…" She bent down, and Jodie could smell that, too—flour and vanilla and peaches. Mom must be making a pie.

She picked up the baby, cradling DJ's head against her shoulder. Dev loosened his supporting grip and she saw him rake his lower teeth across his top lip in a gesture of unspoken frustration. There were so many pairs of arms in this little baby's life, reaching out to her.

"Let's bring her bassinet inside," Mom said. "It's getting too hot out here now. Maybe she could lie on her blanket on the lounge-room floor and have a kick. She loves that. I'll get her baby gym, too. She was really hitting those rattles the other day."

"Thank you, Mom," Jodie said.

Just as had happened last night, Dev didn't say a word.

Chapter Six

"Is there anything more you want to talk about at this stage, Jodie?" asked Dr. Reuben on Tuesday morning.

Everyone waited for her response. Mom, Dad, Elin, Jodie's physical and occupational therapists, the neurologist and the obstetrician who'd delivered DJ nearly twelve weeks ago.

And Dev.

DJ herself was at home with Lisa. She and Elin were both schoolteachers, with the summer off, which Mom had pronounced to be a blessing. Jodie wasn't so sure. Dev seemed restless about the baby's absence, moving as if his empty arms needed filling, although Jodie herself had agreed there was no point in bringing the baby in for this meeting.

"No, I think I'm fine. For now," she said brightly. "I mean, you've all said I can call, talk to anyone about anything at any time. You've said—" she turned to the obstetrician, Dr. Forbes "—that my body recovered very well from the birth itself, and that there's no reason why I shouldn't conceive again in the future."

She bit her lip. Why parrot this back to him, this reassurance about her future fertility, when she hadn't even begun to deal with the baby she already had? She couldn't think of the right things to say. She couldn't think of *anything* to say.

"You're doing very well indeed," the man said.

He was older and a little distant, somehow exactly the kind of man you would expect to have delivered a baby you'd had no knowledge of until two days ago. The kind of man who would have looked after Jodie's physical well-being perfectly and professionally during and after the birth, but who would be rather glad that her emotional adjustment now was an issue for other professionals, such as Dr. Reuben, to deal with.

She felt stubborn and protective and private about it, suddenly. She didn't want professionals helping her to learn to love and take care of her baby, she wanted to do it, like a three-year-old, All By Herself.

Even though she'd already proved to herself that she didn't know where to start.

Trish and Lesley, the therapists, began to speak, stressing the importance of keeping her rehab on track in other areas. It couldn't all be about the baby. Jodie would have to put her own needs first. "It's what they say on airplanes," Trish said. "First, fit your own oxygen mask, then assist your child. If you're not taking care of yourself, how are you going to look after a baby?"

They all seemed to feel that this was a huge risk, that Jodie's own therapy would be derailed by her tiring herself out with her child, attempting one hundred and ten percent.

"I have plenty of help," she managed to say. "I think I'm going to be sensible about it. I know how much love DJ already has, even without me."

Trish and Lesley seemed to approve. Then Trish repeated, "But is there anything more you need? Anything you want?"

Anything I want? Anything I need? I want to love my baby. I want to be the one who knows when she's hungry or tired or hurting. I want to be the one who can soothe her to sleep. I want her to know in her bones that I'm her mom, but she doesn't know it and I don't know how to teach her. She responds to Dev and Lisa and Elin and Mom but not to me, and I'm scared about that.

So scared, she couldn't begin to express it, especially not with all these eyes fixed on her face—the professional gaze of the therapist, the more personal ones belonging to Dev and Mom, trying to hide their concern but without success. Her whole life felt wrong and mixed-up, compared to last fall, before the accident. She remembered one of her last horseback rides, a trail ride through the woods belonging to Oakbank Stables with some intermediate riding students, the hooves of the horses soft on the carpets of newly fallen leaves.

That day, everything had seemed right with the world. The sweet secret of Dev and their plans to see each other that night. The fresh, peaty smell of the woods. The clink of stirrups and bridles in time to the rhythmic movements of the horses.

"I need to see my horses," she said.

It wasn't what Trish or Lesley had expected. Dev and Mom, maybe, but even they didn't understand, she could tell. They thought she had her priorities all wrong. Horses, when she had so much work to do on her body? Horses, when she had a baby to learn to love and care for?

Dad shifted in his seat, and made a gruff sound, but said nothing. He could take her side sometimes, but when he stayed silent, she never knew what he was keeping back. Approval? Or the reverse?

So she backpedalled, ashamed and guilty and scared. "Not yet, of course. I mean, I know that. It's not a priority. But when it happens, it'll do me a world of good, I know it."

"We'll certainly work toward it," Trish promised. "Hippotherapy is a definite possibility for you, given your background." She looked at Dev and Mom, who both nodded. "But that's not what we're here to talk about today."

Jodie understood that she'd gone off-topic, that her therapists and doctors were focused on her adjustment to the baby and the fact that she'd given birth. "I—I really can't think of anything else for now," she told them lamely.

Dr. Reuben and Dr. Forbes both shifted in their seats just the way Dad had, busy schedules dictating that they make a move to the next patients on their lists.

"Thank you," Jodie said to them, and everyone stood up.

Thank you was incredibly useful, she'd begun to discover. You could make it mean so many different things. You could fob people off with it and they never guessed. She thanked Mom for the spreadsheet she'd printed out, even though they weren't sticking to it. She thanked Lisa for her words of experience regarding diaper rash, even though she—Jodie—hadn't done a diaper change yet. You could use it as a piece of very effective camouflage against revealing what you really felt.

The fear.

The doubt.

The distance.

The shame.

She said it again, just to make sure. "Thank you." And everyone nodded and smiled and murmured and told her she was doing incredibly well.

For the next three weeks and more, *thank you* worked like a charm.

She said it to Dev when he picked her up and took her to the park with DJ and did all the carrying in the baby swing and the strapping in and out of the stroller so that Jodie barely needed to touch the baby—or Dev himself—at all. She said it to Mom and Lisa and Elin when one of them took her to rehab while another took care of DJ at home. She said it to Dad when he carried DJ in her car seat or filled her little plastic bath.

Maddy called from Cincinnati to suggest coming up with Lucy for a mommies-and-babies play date, and Jodie said that rehab didn't leave enough space in the schedule right now, but thank you for thinking of it, it was a great idea for sometime down the track. Trish said that Jodie could have the baby at rehab sometimes and they could work on some strategies for taking care of her safely within Jodie's current limitations. Again Jodie hid behind "thank you" and "down the track."

If anyone noticed that she'd only actually held DJ in her arms twice since that first time on the deck, they didn't comment. DJ commented, in her own way. She didn't smile. If anyone noticed that both those smile-less times Jodie had to fight an overwhelming feeling of distance and inadequacy and panic, they didn't comment on this, either.

Or not to her face, anyhow.

Three weeks and four days after her discharge from the hospital, a Wednesday, she caught them commenting behind her back. She'd been taking a nap—this napping business was getting old fast—after a tiring but encouraging day at rehab, when she heard the front door open and the voices of Dev, Lisa and Mom. Moving with the necessary slow precision across her bedroom rug and into the carpeted corridor, she was too quiet and they didn't hear her. She'd only been asleep half an hour, a shorter time than usual. They wouldn't expect her to surface for another hour.

It was the same old line, from Lisa. "I just don't think she's ready, that's all."

"But what's going to make her ready, Lisa?" Dev's voice, low and intense, an emotional, threatening growl that did something to Jodie's insides every time she heard it. "Do you think I was ready, when DJ was newborn? I'd never held a baby in my life. Isn't it only doing it, doing the hands-on with no one to step in the moment you have the slightest episode of not coping, that makes you ready as a parent? You do it, you have to do it and you learn. You live it, you can't imagine life without it and the love kicks in."

"The love?" This was Mom. "She loves DJ! Of course she does! You can't be seriously suggesting she doesn't love her own baby, Devlin!"

"I'm not sure that you're letting her love her, Barb."

"That's not true!"

"I appreciate that she mustn't be overloaded, but do you ever let her feed DJ? Or hold her in the bath?"

"That's not the point!"

Jodie stood with her hands on the stair rail for support, hearing it all. She wanted to tell Dev that it wasn't

Mom's fault. She wanted to say, "Hey, I'm here! Let's discuss this face-to-face, not when you think I'm asleep because you think I can't handle it."

But maybe they were right. She couldn't handle it. She wasn't handling it. The love hadn't kicked in.

"She's working too hard on her rehab, for one thing," Lisa said. "You know what she's like. One of her riding instructors, when she was about twelve, said she had more guts than a slaughterhouse."

"Oh, Lisa!" Barb wailed.

"Yeah, graphic image, but I'll never forget that and it's true. She's an incredibly brave person, and she's exhausting herself with work on her exercises."

"Because she wants to be strong enough to take care of DJ," Mom argued. "Which she isn't, right now. She's told me. She's afraid of letting her fall."

"She's too tired to take care of DJ." Lisa again. "She needs a break, just some time out. From everything."

"I think you're right," said Mom. "Time out. How can we do this?"

"Dev, leave the baby here and just take her out tonight, or something," Lisa said. "Take her to dinner. Take the pressure off. You want her to take more of the load off your hands—"

"It's not about the load," he interrupted. "Do you think that's what this is about? That I want to be able to hand DJ over to her and get the hell out? Shoot, that's the opposite of what I want!"

"I'm not saying that." Lisa stopped, then added in an abrupt tone, "Well. I don't know. You're going back to New York, aren't you?"

"Look, that's a decision I can't make yet."

"You had made it, I thought."

"When we weren't certain she'd ever come out of

the coma. When she was so sick. Of course I wasn't going back to New York if I had a daughter to raise on my own. The situation's changed now, hasn't it? Everything's negotiable. All I know is, I'm not going to be shut out."

"Okay, but I'm assuming—" She cut herself off again. "I don't want to pressure you about the status of your relationship when it's none of my business."

Dad passed through the hall at that moment, and offered, "You got that right!" before he kept right on going, on his way out to mow the lawn.

"It is our business!" Mom said. "It's about DJ's future, and Jodie's well-being. Is there a relationship, Dev?"

"Of course there is. We're the parents of a child."

"You know that's not what I mean."

"Yes, I know it, but that's the only answer I can give you right now."

"We're going around in circles." Lisa gave a sigh that traveled all the way up the stairs to Jodie on the top landing.

"We are," Dev said. "But taking her to dinner is a good idea, and I'm happy to do it."

Lisa kicked into action at once. "I'll make a reservation. How far are you willing to drive? There's that gorgeous new French place in Fairfield—La Brasserie. If you cut across through the back roads, it's not too far."

"And I'll run DJ's bath," Mom said. "By the time Jodie wakes up, she can have the bathroom to herself to take a shower and get ready. It's still early. If you make the reservation for seven, Lisa. That way Jodie's not out too late."

"Isn't La Brasserie a little too—?"

But they didn't let Dev finish. "Make it special,"

Lisa insisted. "Make it a milestone. A new start. She's off the walking frame. She's already so much stronger and better than she was a few weeks ago. She knows we're here for her. And she's always fought so hard to be independent and to achieve her goals. If she's not fighting us for more hands-on with DJ, it's because she doesn't feel it would be safe. When she's ready, I know my baby sister, she'll say so! She'll absolutely insist!"

Thank you, Lisa.

Was it true, though? It would have been true, before the accident, Jodie knew. Now, though… Would she absolutely insist?

"You're right," Mom decreed. "She will."

Jodie started carefully down the stairs. "Are you guys making plans for me?"

Mom looked up at her. "Oh, you're awake already?"

"Just now. It's great, isn't it? Down to one nap, most days, and it's getting shorter."

"We're sending you and Dev out to dinner," Lisa said. "DJ's staying here."

"Can I help with her bath?" She caught the covert, meaningful looks Mom and Lisa exchanged that seemed to say, "See? Jodie's absolutely insisting."

"Of course, honey," Mom said.

But they didn't let her, not really. Dev went home to shower and change. Lisa made the restaurant reservation. "La Brasserie, Jodie, it's gorgeous. You wouldn't have been there, since it's new." Mom ran the water, testing it expertly with her elbow to make sure it wasn't too hot.

"Let me get her undressed," she said, "because that's tricky."

Jodie stood back and watched as the little wriggly arms came out of the stretch cotton dress, looking so fragile and small and wobbly it seemed as if one wrong move from Mom's expert hands and the arms might break.

Jodie hissed in a horrified breath at the mental image and Mom turned to her with a question in her face.

"It's okay," Jodie said quickly. "Just glad you're doing this bit."

But then Mom did the next bit as well, sliding DJ into the bath and scooping the warm water over her perfect, satiny, slippery skin.

"Doesn't she ever smile in the bath?"

"Ooh, no, bath is way too serious for that," Mom cooed, gazing down at DJ, her own smile as gooey as a marshmallow. "She used to shriek, at first, but she likes it now. Don't you, sweetheart precious?"

"H-how can you tell, without her smiling?"

"Look at her splashing her little arms and wriggling around." Mom was still beaming, her hair damp around her face, a damp patch on the front of her blouse and two pink spots on her cheeks. She looked as happy as a young girl, but she also looked deeply tired. She was sixty-five years old, with forty years as a parent and seventeen years as a grandmother already under her belt. How much longer could she keep this up?

I have to start learning.

"Could I shampoo her hair?"

"Of course." Mom took a step to the side. She kept hold of DJ, while Jodie pooled a tiny amount of baby shampoo onto the round head with its water-slicked hair. She massaged it in, her coordination still jerky. Mom cradled the little head in her cupped palm to keep it steady.

"I don't think I'd better rinse it off," Jodie decided. "I might get shampoo in her eyes."

So Mom did that part, also, then picked her up and wrapped DJ in a towel and sent Jodie for a clean outfit and a fresh diaper. "Just one of her little playsuits, in the second drawer. This is what Maddy used to do for you when you were newborn and she was seven, choose your outfits after your bath."

Great, Jodie thought. *My child-care capabilities are those of a seven-year-old. I'm so proud.*

But it wasn't funny. It hurt. It shook her up. And she couldn't talk about it because that would only shake her up more.

Dev appeared at six-thirty, because Fairfield was a half-hour drive away. Jodie had spent nearly an hour getting ready, and in this area there was genuinely something to celebrate because she didn't need help with any of it now. She could get her arms into both sleeves. She could manage the whole shower. Lipstick and mascara were another story, but this was easily solved. Her face was cleansed, exfoliated and moisturized, but makeup-free.

She met him at the front door and his expression seemed to approve the swirly print dress and tiered jacket, which she had teamed with flat shoes in basic black because managing killer heels at this stage would have made managing lipstick seem easy. He looked so good himself, in dark pants and a lightly patterned button-down shirt, freshly shaven and his hair still a little damp around his neck from the shower.

They'd both dressed as if it were a date, she realized. Was it a date?

But no, they'd answered that one already.

"How's DJ?" was the first thing he said to her.

"Oh, great. Asleep. I gave her her bath. Well, helped."

"Did you?" She could tell he was pleased, and felt

guilty that she'd overstated her involvement. What was that really about? Wanting to make him happy? Or hiding her own distance and fear?

He put his arm around her back as they walked to the car. To an outsider they would have looked like a standard pair of new parents, taking a well-earned break for couple time while Grandma babysat. It was such a long way from the truth. Such a long, long way.

Dev had a glass of red wine with his meal but Jodie kept to plain water. "I'm not putting anything into my body that's going to interfere with my control."

It made sense, yet still he told her, "You can let go a little, can't you?"

The idea of this evening had been to relax her, but so far it hadn't worked. He could see her intense concentration on managing the meal, to the point of twisting the pepper grinder over her chicken all by herself when the waiter was eager to do it for her.

He could see her making the right kind of conversation, too, refusing to rehash today's milestones in rehab and instead dragging in current events and politics and celebrity gossip as if this were a neurological examination. Could she remember the name of Scarlett Johansson's latest film? Could she keep track of this summer's star players in baseball and golf?

"I want to progress," she answered.

"You won't, if you push too hard. You'll get overloaded and go backward. Was this dinner a mistake?"

"No, it's great." She squeezed out a smile.

"It's not what you need," he said on her behalf, because he could suddenly see this, and knew she wouldn't say it herself.

"No, you're right, it's not." Her face fell. "I thought maybe it was, but   "

"I'm sorry. It was Lisa's idea, and I know how much she cares about you and wants you to get strong."

"They all care about me. It seems to blind them, sometimes. It's always been this way, and it's so hard to fight it when I'm fighting with everything I have just to use a damned fork without messing up!"

She blinked back tears of anger and frustration and all he could think was *Hell! Hell!* Out loud he said, "But that's them. Your family. This is me. You can tell *me* what you really want and need, can't you?"

There was a pause and he could see her struggling, pushing things back deep inside. A familiar fear surged inside him. What might she say? What would he do if she wanted him out of her life completely?

She had no right to insist on it, since he was DJ's father, but how much of a battle did he want, with his innocent daughter as the winner's prize? Would he take her to family court over it? Hell, he dreaded anything like that. He knew that the law could make custody issues worse as well as solving them, especially when the matter crossed state lines.

She pressed her lips together and he knew she'd decided to keep something back, and yet when she spoke, he could see it was going to be important and honest, even if it wasn't the whole truth. "I want to go to Oakbank. I want to see the horses. And ride. People are acting as if that's something trivial, something to think about down the track, but it's not, it's something I want now. It was so much a part of my life. Way more a part of my life than—" She stopped, flooded with color and pressed her lips together again.

He understood and said it for her. "Than being a mom. Because you weren't one."

"I l-love her."

"I know you do. Of course you do." How could she not? He loved her to pieces.

"I want to take care of her, but I'm scared, and Mom and my sisters… They're so experienced with babies. I need to go back to something I used to do well. Even if I can't do it well anymore, I just need to…be a tiny bit of that person again, for a while, or else I can't learn— I won't learn to be the new— This doesn't make any sense."

Oh, but it did. Shoot, it did. Dev felt he'd been blind, and fallen into the same trap as her family. Not really listening. Not seeing her real needs. "I'll take you tomorrow," he said.

"It doesn't have to be—"

"Tomorrow," he insisted. "We can spend the whole day there, if you want."

"Rehab—"

"Rehab can wait. This is rehab. I'll call Trish and tell her what's happening. I'll call my office and have Marcia cancel my appointments for the whole morning. No arguments, okay, Jodie?"

But she wasn't planning to argue. Her face had lit up. Her eyes were shining. "Thank you, Dev. Thank you so much for not being like my mother and my sisters." She had some color back in her cheeks now that she'd been able to spend a little time outside and the contrast of that smile and that skin and that blond hair took his breath away.

He remembered the way she'd felt leaning against him a few weeks ago, the first time she'd held their baby, so warm, so focused, yet shaky and uncertain, bringing out a kind of tenderness in him he'd barely known could exist. If he could have cut off his own leg to have her fully healed and complete and strong the way she used to be, he would have done it.

"You're welcome," he said, and she must have heard the huskiness in his voice.

Chapter Seven

Driving to the restaurant, the summer evening had still been bright and hot, but now it was dark, a kind of misty blue darkness with a big yellow moon rising in the east. The last time she'd been out driving with Dev in open country in the dark, Jodie realized, was the night of the accident. Oddly, she wasn't scared about it. Maybe because she had no memory of the accident or the drive.

They came around a swoopy bend, the same kind of bend they must have come around that night, with forest on both sides. An oncoming car swept past them, going fast. She heard Dev swear beneath his breath. He was thinking of that night, also.

"Do you remember it?" she asked him. "I mean the—"

"I know what you mean. Yes, I remember it. I was conscious the whole time. Let's not talk about it."

"You were thinking about it."

"Can't help it, sometimes."

"Like now, when someone speeds past the other way."

"Yes." Gritted teeth.

Oh, Dev. It shocked her to think of how much he'd been through. She hadn't thought of it this way before— that her long sleep had been a protection, in many ways, while Dev had suffered through the accident, suffered the agony in his leg echoing the agony of uncertainty, not just for that one terrible night, but for months afterward. Would there be a healthy baby? Would the baby's mom ever wake up?

She put her hand on his arm. Ole Lefty, which wasn't always fully responsible for its actions. She pressed and gripped too hard, and he took his eyes off the road to look at her, and slowed the car. She could see the suffering in his face, the surge of memory. His hands were clenched and shaking on the wheel.

A turning appeared just ahead, a side road with a sign that shone brightly when the car headlights hit it. *Deer Pond Park*. He took it without a word and slowed even more, taking his foot off the gas pedal as if he didn't trust himself with the vehicle's power.

The parking area was deserted. The car rolled to a stop in the farthest corner, with Dev's arms slumped over the wheel. The engine died. "I'm sorry," he said, his voice thick as if he was fighting nausea. "It just…hit me. Hell, I'm shaking. And when that car just now— It wasn't even really speeding. It was a family minivan, for heck's sake."

"I shouldn't have talked about it."

"It wasn't your fault. I was thinking about it already. It's the first time I've driven on a dark country road."

"In so long?"

"Couldn't drive at all for the first few months, because of my leg. Since then, I've been pretty busy sticking close to town." Taking care of a baby. Watching her mom wake up.

"I'm an idiot."

"No." He shook his head, ran a still-unsteady hand down his face as if to wipe the emotion away.

"I am. 'It's not always about you, Jodie,'" she said out loud, with bitterness, mocking herself.

Dev opened the car door. "I need some air. For a minute. But this is not your fault. Let's not do that to each other."

He slid out into the fresh night air, walking away from the vehicle, lacing his fingers behind his head so that his elbows stuck out. She heard him breathing, big whooshes of air blown out through rounded lips. He circled back and leaned his thighs against the hood of the car, looking out over the moonlit pond just yards away, still blowing those careful breaths.

She scrambled out of the vehicle and went to him. "Dev…"

"You were lying there," he said, the words torn from him as if by a force he couldn't control. "I could barely reach you to touch. Just my fingertips. Couldn't do anything for you. I could see blood in the dark. I could hear the other driver yelling and moaning. Crying on the phone when he got himself together enough to call 911. I didn't know… I thought you were breathing but I wasn't sure. And my leg was trapped. And shattered. They had to cut us out. It took three hours."

"Oh, Dev…"

"I'm sorry." He pressed his fingers into his eyes. "Your family didn't want me to tell you all that."

"No. They wouldn't."

"I'm sorry."

"Don't do that to me, Dev, don't treat me like a child, the way they do. I'm not. I'm a grown woman. A strong woman. And I'm— I'm—" She didn't know how to finish.

In your debt, forever.

Here for you, forever.

Words weren't strong enough.

Touch just might be.

She reached for him, running her stronger right hand—the one that she might actually be able to control—up his arm. She rested it on his shoulder, beside his warm neck, and leaned her body close. "You're amazing," she said. "You've carried this load of memory all on your own, while I've been free."

"I guess I did need to talk about it." He was still shaking a little, not from weakness, she guessed, but from the effort of holding everything in. She didn't want him to hold it in. Such tightness and control would surely kill him.

Let go, Dev, let go.

Not fully aware of what she was doing, she began to soothe his muscles with her touch, the way her own muscles had been massaged back into life with physical therapy. She knew all those movements so well, by now.

That's better. That's good. Let go, Dev.

He let out another shuddering sigh and wrapped his arms around her. She felt the warmth of the car hood from the hot engine, and heard it begin to tick as it cooled.

"When the paramedics arrived and confirmed you were alive, this rush of relief, I can't describe…" His voice rumbled against her chest, his breath making a heated caress in her ear. "And then they gave me drugs for the pain and I had this hallucination. I thought we were in a shipwreck, floating in a lifeboat with sharks circling in the water, the only two people left in the whole world. All I could reach was your hair. I held on to it...."

He showed her, taking a soft handful in his fist. She could feel his thumb resting, light and warm, on the back of her neck. He moved a little, bringing his cheek against hers. It was a little rough, so familiar, so good. She turned her head and pressed her lips there, because she couldn't stop herself. He sighed and she felt his mouth against hers, kind of soft and absentminded as if he weren't really here. He was still back in that horrible night.

"That was all I could reach," he repeated. "And then they cut you free and took you away. And it was just me and the sharks." He laughed.

"Wasn't funny at the time," she whispered.

"Nope."

"Wish I'd been there."

"I'm glad you weren't."

"Well, I'm here now." She took his face in her hands, and her hands did what they were told as if they wanted this, too. She pressed her lips to his forehead and then— because she couldn't help it, she was so overwhelmed with feeling for him, with a sense of all the power that connected them—to his mouth.

Oh, Dev. Oh, Dev.

He kissed her back, hungry about it, desperate. His mouth was almost too hard against hers, and he crushed the breath out of her lungs, leaning into her. She had to ease him away, but, oh, not too far.

Yes, Dev, if kissing you helps to let go...

I'll kiss you for whatever reason you want, for every reason there is.

Their two mouths melted together once more, sweet with the chocolate that had finished off their meal. He let go of her hair and moved his hands down to cradle her backside and pull her closer, the swirly skirt of her dress falling against his legs.

She could feel his arousal and he didn't try to hide it. He wanted her to know what was happening, and he couldn't be in any doubt, himself, about what this was doing to her. Her body came alive, her senses reborn. Even the texture of his shirt seemed magical. The woodsy male smell of him. The dark fan of lashes against his cheek that she glimpsed when her eyes drifted open.

She touched him, her hands not fully controlled so that sometimes her grip wouldn't let go or her hand would land in the wrong place. There weren't any wrong places, really. Everywhere felt right. His hip, the top of his thigh, his shoulder blade.

And then it got serious.

He slid his hands beneath her top to touch her bare skin and she wanted those hands on her breasts. He must have known. He dragged his mouth away from hers and trailed it down, pulled her summery jacket from her shoulders and traced the neckline beneath it with his lips. The straps of her top and cream lace bra fell against her upper arms.

He lifted her breast in his cupped palm and breathed a warm breath against her peaked nipple, ran his tongue around it and sucked, released, kissed, sucked again. A fire of pleasure and need stabbed down into her groin, and her body told him *keep going, we are so good at this, both of us.*

She reached for the fastening of his pants, but couldn't make her fingers work. They scrambled help-lessly and in the end she just left them there, curled against his stomach, while she kissed her way down his chest then pushed her forehead into the hard, flat place between his hips. Through the textured fabric of his pants, she felt the push of his erection against her mouth.

"No…" he groaned, pulling her up. "I want you closer."

"That's not close?"

"I want you like this.…" He pressed himself into her, kissed her mouth again.

"Yes, oh, yes." She tried his fly again and did better this time. The button came through the hole, the zipper eased down.

"We can't do this," he muttered, but he didn't mean it.

"I want to." She always did, when it was Dev. Al-ways. Something about him. No explanation. Just chem-istry. "Do you?"

"Hell, do I? How can you ask?" He straightened from his lean against the car hood and flipped her around in one twirl of a movement so that she was the one lean-ing. The engine was still warm. He cupped her bottom again and lifted her higher until she sat on the smooth metal. "It's not going to be pretty."

"I don't care."

"Good. Neither do I."

Maybe it wasn't pretty, but it was beautiful—dark and moonlit and beautiful. He grew patient, as if there were no hurry in the world now that they'd agreed on what they wanted, and just kissed her for a long, long time. Her mouth. Her shoulders. Her breasts. Touching her everywhere. Teasing her deliberately until she was almost whimpering, wanting him so badly, swollen with it, more than ready.

Of his own readiness, there was no doubt. His erection nudged at the apex of her spread thighs, hard and hot. She wrapped her legs around him and he slid her skirt until it bunched at her waist, then pushed aside the triangle of fabric at her crotch. They were doing this fully clothed, and that was just fine.

Fully clothed.

He had his wallet in his back pocket and it carried protection. She held him while he rolled it in place, running her fingers over the taut skin across his lower stomach, brushing the small, tight buds of his nipples through his shirt.

When he entered her, she was as smooth as silk around him, tight with her own need and he filled her so completely that she gasped at the first thrust. Oh, Dev. Oh, Dev. Yes. She clung to him, legs and arms shaking with effort, and he guessed it would have to be quick or not at all.

The car rocked and Jodie sobbed. He pinned her with his hands, stroked her with his hardness until the night exploded. She was a little ahead of him and took him with her, shuddering with gut-deep sound.

Yes. Oh, yes.

They were both breathless. He laughed and held her hard, and maybe she should say something. *That was amazing.* But it seemed trite and so obvious. Hell, yes, it was amazing. When had it not been amazing with Dev? So she just laughed with him and kissed him clumsily. He was just as clumsy, kissing her back.

"You can make a man forget, can't you?" he said.

"That wasn't the reason for it."

"No, I know, but it helped. It was good, Jodie."

"Good?"

"Amazing."

He sounded humble, which was how she felt, too. Humble because she didn't know what happened next. Didn't know how to ask. Didn't know *what* to ask.

Are we dating?

They weren't. They'd agreed.

And yet there was this. Stronger than ever.

He'd gone very quiet, very still.

"I'm not allowed to drive yet," she said, even though he knew this perfectly well.

"Are you asking if I'm okay to drive?"

"Don't particularly want to have to call one of my sisters to come with her husband and ferry us home."

"We won't have to do that. Just give me a minute."

"Have lots of them. As many as you like."

"Not too many, or we'll get a phone call asking where we are."

"Mmm, true, and Deer Pond Park probably wouldn't be a good answer."

"No."

They giggled like teenagers, and she thought, just as she'd thought last year, *don't spoil this, Jodie, don't try to nail exactly what he thinks and feels. Life is so precious. You almost had it taken away. Don't spoil this, when it's been...*

Amazing.

Dev made it back to the Palmer home without cracking up at the wheel. His whole body tightened and went on high alert, heart racing and sweat breaking out, every time a car went past, but he made it, breathing out a sigh of gratitude when they left the dark country road and came beneath Leighville's street lighting. He sighed again when he turned into Barb and Bill's driveway.

Jodie fell against him a little as he helped her out of the car. She often did. It was nothing new, something she couldn't help because of that weakened left side of her body. This time, though, he pulled her against him and kissed her sweetly, because he didn't want her to think he'd just closed the book after one quickie on the car hood in a deserted nighttime parking lot.

It wasn't supposed to be a long kiss, but he couldn't help himself. Lied to himself about it, in fact. Told himself it would be just one more moment of sensing her sweetness and grace, just one more moment of smelling her clean skin, tasting her peachy mouth. He didn't intended it to last long. Just one more sweet touch, that was all it would be.

But he couldn't stop. He tried. Took his mouth away in a brushing movement that only made him want to go back again, and go deeper this time.

Oh, so much deeper, the way he had twenty minutes ago in Deer Pond Park.

He ran his hands over her neat, sweet backside, made into the perfect rounded shape from her years of riding. He brushed the undersides of her breasts with his fingers. He slid his thigh between her legs and felt the silky swish of her dress fold around him in a way that mimicked the much more intimate kind of folding he'd so recently known.

It seemed incredible that his need could mount again so fast.

And she kissed him back. There was no doubt in the world about that. She lifted her face, parted her lips, shaped her body to fit against his so perfectly that she could be in no doubt about what his was doing to him. Again.

"One thing my body can still do," she whispered.

"Yes, oh, yes," he whispered back, his voice raspy with need. "You hadn't been scared about that before tonight, had you? Scared that it couldn't?"

"I hadn't thought. I hadn't considered—"

"Of course you hadn't." He brushed her mouth again, teased her lips with his tongue, cupped her head in his hands.

But the moment had changed. The whole Palmer family was inside the house, and Jodie had remembered the fact. She hadn't asked Dev what it all meant, back at the park, and he was glad about that because he wouldn't have known what to tell her.

"This isn't a good idea right now," she said.

"I'm sorry."

"It wasn't just you."

"I started it."

"I let you."

"You're not really strong enough yet to push me away."

"Oh, you think?" She did it with a cheeky smile, a nice shove to his chest—a little clumsy but very well-directed—and began to steer herself firmly toward the house, the shoe sole on her weaker side brushing the paving with a light rasping sound.

The front door opened, and Barbara appeared. For a moment, Dev wondered if she might have seen that steaming kiss. Lord, he shouldn't have let himself! It should never have happened! It hadn't *needed* to happen when he'd kissed her so thoroughly—and done so much more—in the moonlit park.

But Barb's face seemed untroubled, and he had no

doubt that she would have looked and behaved differently if she'd been watching them from the window. "Elin said you were home. You're a little later than we expected. How did it go, honey?"

"Major victory with the pepper grinder. Slightly challenging drive home in the dark, on the country roads. That's why we're home late. We took it slow."

Some of it they took slow, Dev amended to himself, fighting back his awareness of everything she hadn't said. Some of it they took at magical, erotic speed.

"And I'm cutting class tomorrow," Jodie finished.

"Cutting class?"

"Dev's taking me—" She stopped and corrected herself. "Dev's taking *us* to Oakbank."

"Us?"

"Me and DJ." Her voice wobbled a little at the end, and there was a little note of triumph in it, too. Dev heard it, and was so happy she wanted to bring the baby, too.

Barb looked at him. "Dev?"

"I think it's a great idea," he said firmly. But he knew from Barb's face that she wasn't going to let him off the hook that easily.

Chapter Eight

Elin appeared at Dev's front door just as he was about to head upstairs to bed, after some mindless TV to wind himself down. For the first three seconds, he thought it was about DJ and the strength drained from his legs. It was after eleven at night. His little daughter had been fast asleep an hour ago when he'd left the Palmers, just a few blocks away.

But this was anger on Elin's face, not panic. "We need to talk," she said.

She was a strong woman, a good six inches taller than Jodie and more heavily built, with the weight of her three children starting to gather around her hips. She had Jodie's blue eyes, blond hair and wide smile and Dev liked her a lot, but he didn't particularly want her here on his doorstep with such a hostile look on her face, and arms folded in a way that said she meant business.

"Come in." What else could he say?

She launched in before she'd even crossed the threshold. "I heard your car in the driveway. I was in DJ's room picking up a load of laundry. I looked out the window to see how Jodie was managing the climb from the car. And I saw what happened." The accusation was crystal clear.

"Right," he answered. What would she say if she knew what had happened half an hour before that? He shuddered to think. "Would you like coffee, or something?"

"No, I wouldn't. I'd like to know what the hell you think you're doing with my sister."

Pretty obvious, wasn't it?

Unfortunately, however, Elin was right. He knew it as he'd known it all along. He hadn't absorbed a second of the TV murder mystery he'd just watched, because he'd been thinking about tonight instead. He should never have kissed her, let alone sat her on the hood of his car, pushed her pretty skirt up to her hips and—

Yeah.

Had that shattering episode of flashback to the accident done so much to destroy his good sense? Or was that only an excuse?

He sighed between his teeth. "Okay, you don't have to tell me."

But Elin told him anyhow. "She is so vulnerable right now! She has so much to deal with and to work out."

"Don't I get a share in that?"

"A share in what?"

"The vulnerability, the stuff to deal with."

"All the more reason I shouldn't have to say this, Dev. You have no right to add any kind of complication whatsoever, and especially not that kind. Can you honestly tell me she's in the same place she was in last year—or that you're in the same place—when it was okay for both of you to have a no-strings-attached relationship with a use-by date of three months? Can you honestly tell me DJ doesn't make a massive difference to the equation?"

"No, I can't. You're right."

"Are you going back to New York?"

"You'd like me to, wouldn't you?"

"What makes you say that? Is that an accusation?"

"I guess it is, Elin. I think you and Barb would sometimes be only too happy to have me out of the picture, now that Jodie's recovering, because it would simplify everything, wouldn't it?"

"It would, if you're going to start messing with my sister's emotions. I'm not having that, Dev, I'm just not. Are you in love with her?"

"Don't ask me that."

"I'm her sister and I care about her."

"It's not fair. You're right, we shouldn't have kissed. And yes, I'm phrasing it that way because you must have seen that she kissed me back." *And if you could have seen her in the park, gasping when I suckled her breast, arching her back, clinging to me and moaning...*

"She's vulnerable."

"I know. It won't happen again."

It couldn't. It was too big a risk.

That pang he'd felt just now when he thought DJ might be ill... Imagine if Jodie tried to shut him out because he'd slept with her and messed with her emotions and she couldn't forgive. Imagine if he lost his daughter because of one piece of very male loss of control. His whole body ignited in Jodie's arms, but his head and his heart had to rule right now. His body didn't get a vote.

"So you're not in love with her?"

"I don't even know what that means, Elin."

"Sure you do."

"I care about her." Otherwise why the heck would he be busting his gut to help her bond with her baby, when it could so easily backfire on him? It didn't make sense.

"You'd damn well better!"

"We have DJ. I don't want conflict. I want whatever we decide, long-term, to be the best outcome we can find for DJ."

She snorted, part pacified, part bristling and protective. "If I think you're going to hurt her…"

"I would never hurt my daughter."

"My sister. I know you wouldn't hurt DJ. That's the only thing that's stopping me from hitting you right now." She bracketed her hands on her hips. "But if you hurt my sister…"

She didn't finish, and he didn't dare to make a promise he might not be able to keep. Sometimes it just wasn't in one person's power to stop the other person from getting hurt. The idea of hurting Jodie… Well, it hurt *him*, it made his chest go tight and his breath catch. But that didn't mean he had the power to prevent it.

"I hear you, Elin," he said wearily. "You've said the right things. I won't forget. I'm glad you came."

The weather was perfect, with a breeze from the northwest making a rare break in the summer's humidity and heat. Jodie couldn't have wished for a better day. Mom and Elin had both said they wished they could come to Oakbank with her, but they had errands to run this morning and Jodie wasn't sorry. The idea of being alone with Dev and DJ frightened her the way it always did—two very different reasons, there—but it was still less daunting than the prospect of her mother and sister watching her like a hawk the whole morning.

DJ was awake and happy when Dev arrived to collect them, to Jodie's relief. It meant he focused on the baby, on cooing at her and picking her up. It gave both of them a distraction and a way to keep their distance from each other after everything that had happened last night.

The unsuspected vulnerability he'd shown over his memories of the accident. The bone-deep need she'd felt to soothe his fear away. The explosive power of their lovemaking. On the hood of the car, for crying out loud, with both of them climaxing within seconds of each other, not caring that they were right in the open air, not caring about the previous agreement they'd made.

He regretted it.

Every word he spoke and every movement he made telegraphed the fact.

Minimal eye contact.

No touching at all.

When his body softened and his voice went tender, it was because of DJ. When he smiled, he smiled at his daughter, and she smiled back. It was the right thing, Jodie knew, the only thing. She should be grateful for it. Instead, she had to fight not to feel shut out. Still, DJ hadn't yet once smiled for her.

Mom and Dev had a little back-and-forth over whether he'd packed enough diapers, and whether she'd be sheltered enough from the sun. "She's too young for sunscreen," Mom said.

"I have a hat for her," Dev promised, "and the stroller's canopy shades her when she's in that."

"Wipes?"

"Right here."

"Pacifier."

"She doesn't like it."

"You mean you don't like it. You don't believe in them. But I raised all four of mine and they were never too attached—"

"I have a pacifier, Barb," he said patiently, "but she just spits it out again whenever I try it."

"It's not important, is it?" Jodie said, and they both looked at her, their frustration with each other spilling in her direction.

"Ready?" Dev asked.

"More than."

DJ was getting on for four months old now, and growing every day, her periods of alert wakefulness getting longer and her body strengthening as fast as Jodie's. You would scarcely know that she'd been born seven weeks premature. Dev strapped her into the car seat and they were away in just a few minutes, after those first awkward moments, heading west out of town to the rolling green hills where Oakbank's twenty horses grazed.

Their route covered part of the same road they'd taken on the way back from the restaurant last night, but it seemed so different in the daylight, none of the menace and memory, and they turned onto a different road before reaching the sign and turnoff leading to Deer Pond Park.

Oh, Oakbank was so familiar and so well-loved and she'd forgotten so much of it, but it all came flooding back, every fresh sight and sound. The gravel of the long driveway entrance popping beneath the tires, the lush shade of the summer-clothed trees, the white-painted fences, the loom of the big red barn as they turned into the parking area.

Behind the barn, beyond a screen of greenery, was the manager's cottage she'd been living in at the time of the accident. Katrina and her boyfriend had it now, although they hoped to buy their own place soon, apparently. Jodie's family had moved all her things back to Mom and Dad's after the accident because no one had known if she'd ever be able to return to her little home. She'd recovered so much better than they'd all feared, but still it might be a while before she could live independently.

Independently...

On her own?

Her and DJ?

She couldn't picture it, tried to imagine herself and a baby in the manager's cottage, but it was such a scary idea. Her fine motor control would have to improve a heck of a lot before she could even think about it. The thought came with a flood of both relief and guilt.

So don't think about it, Jodie, think about just being here right now instead.

She saw a string of kids on horseback heading out on a trail ride with members of the summer staff at the head and tail of the group, and realized they must be a batch of vacation day-campers. There was another group doing a beginner lesson in the outdoor arena, where morning shadow still stretched across the sand from a line of cool oaks.

Anna and Katrina, the two full-time riding instructors, knew she was coming. Dev had phoned this morning from his place. They came hurrying out as soon as they saw her climb from the car, and she had to blink back tears as she hugged them both.

"Oh, it's so good to see you!"

"We wanted to visit more...."

"We're so glad you're here."

They'd each come to visit her once in the hospital, but hadn't seemed to know what to say. She'd been a little hurt at the time. They couldn't have come more often? They couldn't have stayed longer, and talked more?

Now, of course, she understood how hard it must have been. They'd known about the baby, but couldn't talk about it because of the medical decision that Jodie herself wasn't yet recovered enough to know. She felt their apology about all those unsaid things in the warmth of their greeting, and something inside her eased a little.

"And I'm so glad I've come," she said. "It's the best thing. Do—do you want to see DJ?"

Dev was unstrapping her carrier from the back of the car. She'd gone to sleep, lulled by the journey. "Can we bring her inside first?" he said. "The sun's so bright." He draped a soft flannel blanket over the top of the carrier handle to shade her.

Anna and Katrina led the way, and Jodie almost kept up with them, she felt so strong and energized just by being here.

The barn was cool and quiet, its wide end doors flung open to catch the fresh breeze. Clean sawdust covered the arena, horses poked their heads over the half doors of their stalls and there was Bess, saddled and working, walking patiently down one long side with a child holding the reins and a therapist by her side.

Dev put DJ's car carrier on one of the bleachers that overlooked the arena and took off the flannel blanket. Anna and Katrina both bent over the carrier, clucking and cooing at the sight of the sleeping baby. "It's incredible, Jodie," Anna said.

"I guess it seems so right and natural to you now," Katrina said. "But we're still in shock. She is beautiful."

"And you are amazing."

That word again. Dev had said it last night.

"I don't feel amazing." And if they knew that it didn't feel right and natural at all with DJ, if they knew she still hadn't smiled at her...

"No, you never do," Katrina said, "but trust me, you are."

"Tell me that once I'm in the saddle!"

"You really want to ride?"

"Katrina, have you ever known me to *not* want to ride?"

"Holly's about to finish her session," Anna said. "You're next."

"Oh, that's Holly?" Jodie looked at the girl in the saddle. "Wow, she's grown since I last saw her!"

Holly had cerebral palsy, and had been coming to Oakbank for hippotherapy since she was six years old. She adored her riding lessons, and had shown significant improvement in muscle tone and coordination over the past four years. As always, she slid down from Bess's back wearing a huge smile, put her arms around the horse's neck and kissed her. "I love you, Bess."

Jodie hung back a little, not knowing if Holly would recognize her after ten months of absence and so much change. Her hair was shorter. Her body moved so differently. She was thinner and so much of her athlete's muscle tone had disappeared. Jodie didn't think that she looked actively *scary,* or anything, but still...

"Say hi, Jodie," Dev prompted. "I don't think she's seen you."

"I— Yes, okay. Of course I'm going to say hi. She's a great kid."

But the moment had gone. With the therapist at her side, Holly had started toward the arena's opposite exit where her mother was waiting, already full of news about her ride. "Did you see me trot, Mommy? I was on the correct diagonal the whole time."

Oh, well, there'd be another time. Jodie walked up to the patiently standing horse. "Hi, Bess," she said softly.

Bess turned a big brown eye toward her, and gave a satiny little prod with her nose. Recognition? Probably. Horses had good memories. Jodie rubbed the horsey face gently, fighting to keep her coordination so that it felt good on Bess's shaggy cheek. "There? Is that okay? Is that how you like it, Bessie-girl?"

Katrina brought a mounting block, something Jodie had never needed before. Then, remembering, she proclaimed, "My helmet!"

"Here," said Anna. She'd crossed the soft sawdust with barely a sound. "It's been hanging on the hook behind the office door this whole time."

"Need help?" Dev offered.

"I'm fine." But it was tricky, and in the end she couldn't manage the helmet's plastic catch and had to accept his offer. His fingers brushed her jawline and the tender skin beneath her chin as he fastened the clasp and she closed her eyes, thinking of last night. Was Katrina watching? Could she see…?

See that I'm thinking about kissing him, about feeling him inside me.

It had kept her awake for far too long. The need and wanting. The powerful body memories. The regret. Why had she let it happen? Why had his vulnerability caught so strongly at her heart? Why hadn't she found a different way to respond? How could her awareness of him surge so fast when she had so much else to deal with? It didn't make sense. She didn't want it.

And she didn't want one simple brush of his fingers to take her back to last night with such immediacy and power. The clasp snapped into place and she stepped back, unsteady but very relieved.

"Ready?" Katrina asked.

"Not sure how we do this."

"You've helped other riders a thousand times, Jodie." Kat's voice was an odd mix of deference and encouragement. She was five years younger than Jodie, and had begun working here part-time at seventeen, when Jodie was twenty-two and already a well-qualified riding instructor. Their relationship of mentor and student had changed, too, because of the accident. "You were the one who taught me how to assist a rider with special needs, remember?"

"Different when it's me. Different when my legs don't work right. Can we talk it through?"

"Of course." Katrina talked her through each movement, where each hand and foot went, when she would give a boost.

It felt wrong, and then as soon as she arrived in the saddle, she was at home. "Oh, Bessie, you good girl!"

The horse's broad back was alive and warm beneath the saddle, her mane shaggy in front. Jodie reached forward and ran her fingers awkwardly through it, while the familiar horsey smell rose to her nostrils. "Are you going to lead me, Kat?"

"Yep, if you want."

"I haven't been led on a horse since I was seven years old!"

"Well, I could set up a show-jumping course for you,

with twelve fences and five foot-high rails, but you'll have to give me a few minutes for that."

"Okay, just for you, we'll save that for the next ride," Jodie said.

It was so weird and at the same time so good. Katrina led Bess at a walk, and the horse's rocking rhythm was more even and steady than Jodie could yet manage on her own legs. This was one of the benefits of therapeutic riding. It gave people a sense of the natural rhythm of movement that they might never have experienced on their own.

Soon she was smiling broadly. Her family had never understood her passion for horses. Where had it come from? No one knew. No one else shared it. No cowboys or rodeo riders in the family history, that they knew of. But somehow it was just there, growing in her bones from when she was seven years old and had taken her first pony ride on the woolly back of a chubby Shetland pony.

Sitting on Bess now, she felt like *herself* for the first time since the slow slide out of her coma, and it was so wonderful to discover that the old Jodie still existed somewhere inside her, even if her body couldn't show it yet.

I'm me. I'm still me.

And I'm a mother. I have a baby girl.

"Could DJ come up here with me?" She didn't even think about it, just said it.

The baby was awake now, Jodie knew, because she could hear the start of some little fussing sounds coming from the car carrier. Dev had turned a couple of times to check on her. She was getting bored, all the way over there on the bleachers. Maybe she couldn't see her mommy riding, from so far away, and wanted to take a closer look.

Katrina asked Bess to halt. "Could she? I think it's up to you, Jodie. You know better than me that Bess is the safest horse in the world, and she's not depending on your cues with the reins. You want to sit DJ up there and hold her?"

"Is it okay with you, Dev?" It felt strange to be looking down on him. He stood there, watching her intently, head a little tilted to one side, eyes narrowed. She must have shocked him with the idea of having DJ up on a horse at less than four months old, but not a bad shock, apparently. He was thinking about it, not rejecting it.

Jodie held her breath. *Please agree. Please. Just say yes. Don't question it.*

If he wanted to know why it was so important, she knew couldn't explain in words.

"She does seem to be getting a little bored over there." He'd echoed her own thought. "You think she's going to be a pony gal, like her mom?"

"Hope so!"

He gave a brief nod, didn't say anything out loud, then began walking in DJ's direction. A minute later he'd unstrapped her and brought her over. She was wriggling, sitting up in his arms. She was reaching the same kinds of milestones as Jodie herself. Growing stronger. Becoming more alert.

"How is this going to work?" Dev asked.

"Could you hand her up to me? And then keep ahold of her, just in case? I'll sit her here at the front of the saddle so she's leaning against my stomach. If you just put a hand on her front…"

"Should work," he agreed.

DJ seemed to like the idea. She was waving her arms,

taking happy little breaths and making sounds. Katrina stood beside Bess's head, stroking her nose and cheek and telling her, "You're getting another passenger, but she doesn't weigh a whole lot. Is this a first for you? I think so."

Dev lifted DJ up and settled her against Jodie's front. Jodie wrapped a hand around her middle and found Dev's hand there already, as she'd asked. Their fingers touched and laced together because there was no room for them to do anything else, and the downy back of DJ's little head bumped gently against Jodie's stomach.

With Dev's other arm behind her on the saddle, she felt so close to him. Closer, in some ways, than she'd felt last night with his hands and mouth on her breasts. He could have pillowed his head against her thigh by moving just an inch or two. She remembered what he'd said that first evening at his place, when she'd learned the truth about DJ's birth. *We're a family.* For the first time, with Bess's warm, living strength beneath her, and DJ and Dev both so close, she actually believed it might be true.

"She seems real excited about this," Katrina commented.

"Is she smiling, Kat?"

"No, not smiling, but so alert. Are we standing still, or walking?"

"Walking," Jodie answered. "Ready when you are, Kat. Dev, are you? Will you be able to keep pace in that position?"

"I'm fine. She is really happy, look at her, she's bouncing."

"Still not smiling? I can't see."

"Serious, still, but so eager. You're not missing anything by not seeing her face. It's her body doing the talking."

"Oh, it is, I can feel it. Oh, DJ, you're so happy, aren't you?"

Not smiling, but maybe just as good.

Katrina clicked her tongue and told Bess to walk, and the wonderful rocking motion of the horse began again. Her hooves barely made a sound on the soft sawdust, and when they passed the big open doors where the sun came streaming in, her brown coat gleamed. DJ bounced and made her cooing and gurgling sounds. Dev muttered, "Just managing to keep up, here" beneath his breath, and then, a little louder, said, "She's loving it. Isn't she?"

All Jodie could say was, "Oh! Oh!" Her face hurt from smiling, and her vision blurred with tears.

I'm holding her and it feels right. We're on a horse together and she loves it. She feels like my daughter. My very own daughter. For the first time. I can feel it. I can feel what Dev feels about her. If only I could see her face! That's the only way this could be any better. I never understood. I never knew this was how it could feel.

Oh. Oh.

There were just no words.

I must not let her see how scared I am, Dev thought.

It was perfectly safe. He knew it with his head. His heart couldn't feel it. DJ? His precious baby girl? Fifteen weeks old and on a horse, five long feet from the ground?

But he could see what it was doing for Jodie and that made the fear unimportant. It was such a beautiful sight. Jodie's smile. DJ's excited bouncing, her little mouth open but serious, her hands batting in the air. The horse so slow and steady and patient.

He had to walk almost leaning against the warm equine body in order to keep one hand in place against DJ's stomach. The other hand he rested on the back of the saddle, an inch from Jodie's rounded backside. She'd worn stretchy jodhpurs, sand-colored, because that was what she always wore for riding, and man those things looked good on a woman's body!

His half-side-on position gave him a perfect view of the rhythmic rock of her hips in the saddle, and the only thing that stopped him looking too long and hard and thinking all sorts of forbidden thoughts about last night and those rocking hips on the warm hood of the car was the better view he got from looking higher up, where the big, teary-eyed, dazzling grin on her face just wouldn't go away, and the slight crookedness and lack of control in her arms and shoulders didn't seem to matter at all.

"Oh!" she kept saying. *"Ohh!"* And kind of laughing and crying at the same time, while DJ sat pressed up against her and all that Jodie body language of reluctance about holding and touching her baby had miraculously gone.

He wanted to wrap his arms around her and plant exuberant smooches of congratulation all over her face. *You're amazing!* He wanted to soften those same arms and give her kisses that were tender and wondering and soft on her mouth. *You're amazing.*

This was what he'd been drawn to at eighteen, even though he'd never acknowledged or acted on it back then. This was what still drew him—the combination of fragility and strength, the petite body that had a warrior's fight in it, the determination and perseverance along with a huge, dazzling, sexy smile.

If this was his old life, in New York, he knew what his next move would be. Whisk her away somewhere so that this fizzing need inside him could find a happy release. Ten days in Paris, a three-day weekend in the Bahamas. It had worked for him, in the past.

He always picked the right kind of woman, sophisticated and high maintenance and impossibly well-groomed. Always had a great time, while in the back of his mind—and the woman's—the clock ticked and the objections mounted up.

He couldn't have spent his life with a woman whose grooming rituals took up two hours of every single day. She—a series of them, over the years—couldn't have spent hers with someone who read the international section of the newspaper every day like he was prepping for an exam and then actually wanted to *talk* about it. He couldn't have seriously fallen for someone who paid that much attention to shoes and whose voice went whiny and childlike the moment she didn't get her own way. A few weeks together, though…great.

He'd been smug about it, he now realized. He'd been far too certain and confident about his choices. The right kind of relationship, with the right kind of woman. He'd had it all sewn up, all his bases covered.

Jodie wasn't the right kind of woman.

But she was the mother of his child.

And he'd be stepping back from the whole situation as soon as she was able to take care of DJ herself, as soon as he trusted that they had the right arrangement in place. It was the only thing that made sense. It was— even though they never said it straight out—what her family wanted.

But hell, she looked fabulous up there, grinning from ear to ear, with DJ nestled against her front. He didn't want it to end.

His first inkling of the new arrivals was the sound of Barbara Palmer's voice. "Oh, sweet jeepers, and she has the baby up there, too!"

Before Katrina, Jodie or Dev himself could react, Barb and Lisa came hurrying across the arena. He couldn't see them fully, as Bess's body masked his view, but there could be no doubt about their attitude. Katrina told Bess to halt, which she obediently did, while Jodie had stiffened in the saddle and tightened her arm around the baby.

Dev tightened his own fingers, so that their two hands were knotted tightly together. He felt Jodie squeezing, and squeezed her back. *It's okay, they seemed to be saying to each other. We're in this together, and we're not going to apologize for any of it.* He came so close to laying his cheek against her thigh.

You're amazing....

"It's fine, Mom," she said. "Katrina has the horse, Dev has DJ, nothing bad is going to happen."

"It's not fine! How can you be so irresponsible with your own daughter? How can you even put this as a priority, coming here, at this point in your rehab? Getting on a *horse?* When walking and showering and brushing your hair are still so much of a challenge? How can you?"

"I thought you had errands this morning."

"Lisa called, and I told her you were coming here, and she wanted to take a look. I decided the errands could wait."

"Honey," Lisa said to her sister, "Mom's right, don't you think?"

She was already reaching up, standing on Bess's other side. Dev would have had to fight her for the baby, snatch the little body from Jodie's front with a rough movement, to keep her under his own control. He didn't do it.

"Never mind yourself," Lisa went on, "although that's bad enough. But to put a fifteen-week-old preemie baby on horseback?" She had DJ safely in her arms in a couple of seconds, and began to stroke her silky little head, kiss and hug DJ against her sun-darkened collarbone. She loved her baby niece, no doubt about that. She seemed genuinely shaken by the idea that DJ had been all the way up there on scary Bess's back.

"She liked it," Jodie said.

"Liked it? How could you? Project that onto her? I mean, seriously!"

"We could tell. It was clear."

"You are *projecting,* Jodie. I'm actually pretty angry about this! After we've been so careful, so worried—"

"Lisa, I promise you—"

"Honey, Lisa doesn't mean to sound so—" Barb began, cutting in.

Lisa shook her head back and forth. "Yes. Okay. I'm sorry. Not angry. Just questioning your judgment, okay? And your priorities. Sure, I mean, I guess it sounds great." She mimicked, "'Wow, I was back in the saddle four weeks after I came home from the hospital. My daughter started riding when she was less than four months old.' But it shouldn't be about your ego, should it?"

"It's not about my ego." Jodie's voice had grown strained and tense. The happy grin had gone. And the tears. She was frowning, dry-lipped. "Is that what you think?"

"It's what I thought when you tried to give my Izzy riding lessons when she was three years old. You wanted to turn her into a superstar in a few months, winning ribbons in show-riding competitions and heaven knew what else."

Dev felt his tension level climb as the argument grew more heated. He knew about siblings. He had an older brother in California, a criminal defense attorney, who could still push his buttons when they met up at family gatherings. *Just keep DJ out of it,* he wanted to say, but managed to press his mouth shut.

"That was ten years ago," Jodie was saying, "and I was only just starting out instructing. Izzy didn't like it and so we let it go."

"After she almost fell."

"She didn't *almost*. I had the pony by the bridle and he settled down in about five seconds. I had no idea you were still upset about that, after so long. And it was never about winning ribbons."

"I'm not still upset. I'm not." Lisa shook her head frantically again. "Just seeing you there with DJ reminded me, makes me question what it's really about. Photos for the Oakbank website?" She gestured behind her.

"Photos?" Jodie and Dev both looked where she was pointing, over at the bleachers nearest the office, and discovered Anna there with a camera.

Anna began to walk toward them, her movement a little graceless and awkward as if in apology for the tension she sensed in the air. "I'm sorry, did I do the wrong thing? I didn't want to interrupt and get you to pose, but you looked so great, I just couldn't resist grabbing the camera."

"Great?" Barb exclaimed.

"I didn't know Anna had the camera," Jodie said tightly, then turned to her friend and spoke in a bright tone. "But it's fine. Did you get some? I'd love to see them."

"So they're not for the website?" Lisa persisted.

Dev answered her. "Of course they're not for the damned website! And if they were…"

Had they not seen how Jodie had looked relaxed and happy and *herself* for the first damned time since she'd woken up, how she'd held DJ like a mother for the first damned time since she'd learned the truth about her pregnancy? Had they not even taken a moment to notice any of that before barging in? Would it be such a terrible thing to have a picture of Jodie and her baby girl on the Oakbank website, when she loved the place so much?

"I'm tired," Jodie suddenly announced. "My legs are starting to shake. I think I'd better call it quits for today."

"For today?" Barb wailed.

"Yes, I want to keep doing this. Get better at it. Move on from Bess to Snowy, and see how I go."

"You can't mean you're going to try to ride again the way you used to?"

"You said you hadn't sold Irish."

"Because I knew you'd want to see him. Not *ride* him. You'll never ride him, Jodie."

There was a sharp, painful silence. Dev could have shoved his daughter's grandmother facefirst into the sawdust floor, he was so angry with her. Nobody yet knew whether Jodie's recovery would be complete enough to allow her to ride the way she used to. How could Barb preempt the worst-case scenario like that? How could she shatter Jodie's hopes?

Jodie's jaw set hard and stubborn at her mother's words. "Then DJ will ride him instead. He's only nine years old. She can start on him when she's ten. She'll be a strong rider by then, and he'll be mellow as a lamb at nineteen."

"This is ridiculous," Lisa muttered.

"You got that right," Dev said, his own jaw painfully tight.

It was ridiculous that they'd come. Insane that they were creating conflict out of something that had been so joyful until five minutes ago. Ridiculous and insane and just plain insensitive.

He managed not to say any of this out loud. But he pulled DJ out of Lisa's arms. "I think she needs a diaper change."

"Kat, can you get us back to the mounting block?" Jodie asked in a strained voice.

"Sure, of course. You okay to get that far?"

"I'm fine. As long as Dev has DJ."

"I have her." He turned his back on Lisa and Barb, not certain which of them owned the greater share of his anger. He'd thought of Lisa as an ally, until now. Out of all of the Palmer women, she was the one who was least inclined to underestimate Jodie or overprotect her, the one who might understand that Jodie's bonding with DJ was incomplete and that they might need to try some pretty imaginative strategies to get things on track.

Like putting the two of them up on a horse.

But now he felt betrayed. She was the one who'd gotten Barb's blood up this morning. So Lisa had "wanted to take a look"? Wanted to sabotage the whole event, more like. He didn't doubt that her motives were good. Pristine and pure. She loved her baby sister. Maybe that long-ago episode with Izzy and the riding lessons really did still scare her, even if at heart she knew it wasn't Jodie's fault. The whole family loved her. But boy could love be blind sometimes!

He wanted to tell both women, "You have ruined the best moment Jodie has had since the accident." Even better than last night, because it was right, while last night, in hindsight, probably wasn't. He wanted to say, "You have set her back weeks with DJ. Maybe even months."

And there would be no second chances on those months. They would be the months when DJ would learn to laugh and sit up and look at picture books and maybe even crawl. They would be the months when her sounds would start to mean something to her, and when she would start to distinguish between the faces that looked at her with love and the ones that didn't.

If Jodie lost that little spark of love and rightness that had ignited in her today, when the two of them had sat on Bess together... If it didn't fan into a bright, life-long flame because Barb and frigging Lisa had come along and put it out...

Freaking hell, he would find that hard to forgive.

Chapter Nine

Maybe a real mother, a good mother, wouldn't have done it. Maybe it was the last thing a normal, good mother would have done, asking to have her tiny baby up there with her in the saddle.

Jodie thought about it all day, through the drive home with DJ and Dev, through the tense lunch of chicken salad rolls that her mother made for the two of them after DJ had had her bottle and Dev had gone.

She and Dev had barely spoken to each other in the car, so different from the mood last night when he'd revealed so much and she'd felt so much care. "Are you angry?" she'd asked him.

"Of course I am. Not with you."

She'd wanted him to say more, but he hadn't and she hadn't felt able to push. Angry with Mom and Lisa for interrupting? Angry with them for being right? Angry with himself? He drove less smoothly than usual, those strong hands sliding around the steering wheel, foot stabbing at the brake, eyes unreadable behind his sunglasses.

The powerful body language made her intensely aware of him, the way she'd been up on Bess, with their fingers twined together and his head so close to her thigh. She had to fight not to steal sideways glances the whole time, and itched to touch him, too, to place her hand on his shoulder or his thigh, in an attempt to connect. It wasn't a very obedient hand, though, Ole Lefty. It tended to crab into a tight claw, or twist its fingers at the wrong time. Even if she had dared to touch him, the touch would have turned out all wrong.

He wasn't just angry, but absent. Somewhere else. His thoughts ticked furiously—she could almost hear them—but she didn't know what they were about. They'd almost reached home when she ventured to say, "I guess we'll wait a bit before we try this again."

"Mmm?" Her words had pulled him back from a faraway place, it seemed.

"Before we go back to Oakbank," she explained.

"Look, I don't want to create a rift between you and your family."

"I know. I hate being at odds. They care about me. And they care about DJ."

"Yeah, Oakbank…" He was still deep in his thoughts. Oakbank apparently fit someplace in there, but she didn't know where.

"Well, here we are.…" she told him. Unnecessarily, as he was already turning into the driveway.

And now lunch with Mom, and DJ's spreadsheet-dictated schedule, and a quiet afternoon, when Jodie had half hoped to be at Oakbank most of the day, watching the day campers and group lessons, visiting her favorite horses in their stalls. The whole morning had left a sour taste, far more so than what had happened between her and Dev last night, and she questioned everything about it.

Lisa called in that evening, saying, "I'm sorry," before she'd even entered the house, and they sat in the kitchen together and drank glasses of iced tea. Mom had DJ out on the porch swing at the front of the house, and Jodie could hear the sound of lullaby singing.

"I think I came on too strong this morning," Lisa said. "I know I did. I was just so scared, that's all, when I saw you there, and with the baby."

"I was perfectly safe, Lise. I had Dev and Katrina right by me. Bess has been a fully trained hippotherapy horse for ten years, and she is incredibly well looked after so she doesn't get tired and sour. She is wise and perceptive and calm as a pond. I would trust her with my life."

"We're just a little worried about your priorities, that's all."

"I want to get as strong as I can. I want to put the accident behind me and start being normal again. And riding has always been so much a part of normal for me."

"I just question—" Lisa stopped, huffed out a breath. "Look, I'll just put it out there. How often are you going to blow off your rehab to go to Oakbank?"

"Don't say it that way. I didn't blow it off. Dev called Trish and she thought it was a great idea, as long as I was careful."

"We're just concerned. We care about you."

"I know. Just don't smother me, okay? I hate it."

"Is she fussing tonight? Is that why she's out on the porch swing with Mom?"

130 THE MOMMY MIRACLE

"Um, I think she's fine."

Mom had kept DJ to herself all afternoon, telling Jodie that she needed to rest "after that whole mess this morning." And it was true that she'd felt extra tired, emotional and not as capable as she wanted to be. She'd spent too much time trying to recapture the morning's wonderful, heart-melting sense of certainty about DJ and her own role, but she couldn't. Was it because the mood had been bruised so abruptly? Or was it her own fault?

She didn't want the baby to pick up on all her self-questioning. Horses had such an uncanny instinct about human emotions that they were practically psychic, so why shouldn't babies be the same? It meant something that DJ hadn't yet smiled at her. It hurt her and scared her and she didn't want to make things any worse. So she stayed away, and DJ seemed to have a contented, peaceful afternoon.

Dev hadn't called. The spreadsheet said he was supposed to have DJ overnight today, but the spreadsheet hadn't seen what had happened at Oakbank this morning, so it was even more out of the loop than usual.

"Anyway, I'm sorry," Lisa said again, repeating it and explaining her motives until this, too, felt like a form of smothering.

Mom came into the kitchen with DJ propped on her hip. She rubbed at the small of her back with her free hand as if it were aching, and every pore of her skin looked tired.

"Mom, give her to me," Jodie said, too concerned about that aching back and tired skin to remember her own fears and doubts until after the words were spoken.

Mom shook her head. "It's fine."

"Are you sure?" But, so help her, she felt relieved.

"She'll be ready to go down as soon as she's had her bottle, I think. Dev hasn't called, and he's usually here earlier than this. Is he coming, I wonder? Well, I'm not going to call him. If he wants her, he needs to say so, and if she's down for the night and he shows up, I'm not disturbing her."

"We're all tired," Lisa announced, as if it solved everything.

Dev arrived at the Palmers' twenty minutes too late.

"She's down," Barb told him at the front door. "She went down at seven. Why didn't you call?"

"Because it was already settled that I was having her tonight." He tried to sound patient and pleasant about it, but knew he wasn't succeeding. He gentled his tone further, but still couldn't keep the frustration at bay. "Was she that tired you couldn't have kept her up? It's not like she's asleep at the exact same minute every night."

"You're usually here by six."

"I was…caught up." He'd had a crazy afternoon, getting back to the office to encounter an unexpected crisis with a longtime client of his father's, and then a long call from New York about the international legal case he was supposed to be working on in London in the fall.

The call pulled him back into his work, reminded him how much he enjoyed it. For the first time since DJ was born, he almost forgot her existence, and then he remembered with a flood of conflicting emotion… all that love, all that uncertainty.

He'd spent hours on the phone and at the computer, dealing with the client's problems and the London case while at the same time trying to put a plan in place that he had no intention of sharing with Barbara at this stage.

He just might share it with Jodie's dad, Bill, because occasionally the quiet man gave an inkling that he was more on the ball about Jodie's needs than he let on.

He'd grabbed coffee and a sandwich on the run, had twice been about to send a text to Barb or Jodie to tell them he was running late, but then something else had come up and the text never happened. In the back of his mind, because of Barb's own spreadsheet, he hadn't thought it mattered that much. Now, she'd used a poor excuse yet again to keep DJ under her own roof.

If this was so that Jodie could spend more time with the baby, then he wouldn't have a problem with it, but that wasn't happening. None of the Palmer women seemed to have any thought that Jodie needed help, not with baby-care but with bonding. They were in a state of massive denial, and if he didn't take drastic action soon, then his relationship with the entire family would descend into open conflict.

He couldn't let it happen, because if they or Jodie somehow managed to shut him out of DJ's life... His scalp tightened with dread at the very thought.

"You're not going to wake her?" Barb asked, telegraphing her disapproval very clearly.

"No, I won't wake her. Is Bill around, though?"

"In the basement. Shall I call him?"

"No, I'll go down."

Ignoring Barb's visible curiosity about why he might be seeking out her husband, Dev found him at his workshop bench, planing a curved piece of oak with an old-fashioned handheld plane. Dev couldn't work out what the piece of oak was for, and said so.

"It's the main," answered Bill.

"The main what?"

Bill chuckled. "No, m-a-n-e. I'm making a rocking horse. For DJ."

"Oh. Oh, wow."

They both stood there in a manly silence for several moments, while Dev took in the other pieces of the rocking horse. He began to see how it would all fit together. It was going to be a beautiful piece of workmanship. "I'm not good at the fussy stuff," Bill said eventually.

"This doesn't look fussy at all. It looks…like a piece of art. Incredible."

"I mean the fussy stuff with diapers and bottles."

"Right. You must have done your share."

"When I had to." He chuckled again. "But I like to be involved in my own way. Things like this."

"She'll love it."

"Her first Christmas, I thought. She'll be able to sit on it by then, with help."

"It's going to be really wonderful."

"Going to paint it like Jodie's Irish, dapple gray." He fell silent again, and his laconic manner transmitted itself to Dev, who couldn't find a way to say what he wanted to say. He wasn't even quite sure what he was trying for. In the end it was Bill who helped him out. "I love my wife and my girls," he said, "but it's not going right, is it?"

"No…"

"With DJ, I mean, and Jodie."

"No, I don't think it is."

"Right now, she's everybody's baby, the way Jodie was when she was little, especially after she was ill. She fought it. The horses were the best thing that ever happened to her, although Barb still can't see it. I don't want to watch Jodie hanging back with DJ, not knowing where she fits, not trusting herself with the baby. My wife and my daughters are trying to help, but they're doing it wrong. You can see it, can't you?"

"Yes, I can."

There was another silence. Bill picked up his plane. "Should we get involved?"

"I think we have to."

"Any ideas?"

"That's what I wanted to talk to you about," Dev said.

"And...score!" Trish said.

"Yay, it went in the tub." Jodie clumsily clapped her hands. "That's three times, now."

"Wow, Jodie!" Elin said. She'd dropped in as she occasionally did, to play cheerleader to Jodie's efforts.

Trish moved to retrieve the tennis ball from the big pink plastic bucket, which was about three feet in diameter, six feet away and hard to miss. But the close proximity hadn't stopped Jodie from missing it with the ball about nine times before her first hit. "I'll get it," she said quickly.

"Sure?"

"You and Elin keep scrambling up, and it's good for me to do it, right? Makes the whole exercise more complex and useful." She stood up, walked over, bent down, put in an intense mental effort and got her fingers to close around the ball. Back in her seat, she threw it again—*let go, crazy fingers!*—and there came another rubbery plop as it landed in the bottom of the tub. "Yeah, all right!"

"You're getting much better at this," Trish said.

"Wanna move the tub farther away?" Jodie asked.

"Not today. Practice a little more on your own, if you

want, before we break for lunch. I need to go check on Alice." Trish gestured across to another rehab patient working on a puzzle on the far side of the room.

"Of course I want," Jodie said, and went once again to pick up the ball—before Elin could do it for her.

She threw it, let go at the wrong time and missed by a mile.

She went to retrieve the ball from under the occupational therapy unit craft table—before Elin could do it for her—but someone else had gotten there first.

Dev.

He had a fabric baby pouch strapped over his shoulders, with DJ cradled against his chest.

She went hot and flustered at the sight of them, since Mom's spreadsheet hadn't breathed a word to suggest they were coming. Dev looked somehow formidable today, despite the softening accessory of a baby dressed head-to-toe in pink, right down to a tiny bucket-shaped pink sun hat. His jaw was set, and there was an electricity of intent humming inside him. It flustered her even more, as soon as she picked up on it. "Hi," she said, and asked—before Elin could do it for her—"What are you doing here?"

"It's all okayed with Trish and Lesley."

"It is? What is?" She looked in Trish's direction and received a smile and a thumbs-up in reply.

"Yes, Dev," said Elin, who hadn't been looking at Trish. "What are we talking about?"

"Um, Elin, if you don't mind this is between me and Jodie."

"Well, it isn't, really." She frowned at him. "If you recall our talk the other night."

"Talk?" Jodie came in. "What talk?"

They ignored her. "This has nothing to do with what

we talked about the other night," Dev said to Elin. "I've already agreed you were right about that. So would you mind please—?"

"Butting out? You're telling me to butt out? Mom told me what happened yesterday at Oakbank."

"I told you, too, Elin," Jodie said. "I told you it was great."

Again, they ignored her, glaring at each other, then Dev very deliberately turned in her direction. "I'm a little early, Jodie, because DJ woke up earlier than usual and it seemed best to show up now, before she gets fussy. Ready to go?"

"If you tell me where."

"Can't do that." He picked up her purse.

"Devlin!" Elin said.

"I am not dealing with you right now, Elin. I am not justifying myself to you, or to Lisa, or to your mom. Talk to Trish about it, if you want, but I need to get going before DJ falls apart. Jodie?"

He began to walk toward the door, his stride so long and assured and angry that Jodie had this dizzy, illogical panic that she would never see DJ again if she didn't follow him, so of course she did.

It was as if he had a gun pressed to DJ's head. Or to her own. It was a hostage situation or a kidnapping, he was that cool and controlled and ruthless about it. Elin seemed rooted to the spot. Trish was watching carefully from the far side of the room. When Elin took a pace forward, she called her quickly, and Elin went over to her, chin defiantly raised but ready to listen. A moment later they were in a very female huddle, with Elin nodding and frowning, and Trish persuasively arguing... something.

In a summery skirt and white lacy top, Jodie wasn't

dressed for a kidnapping. In fresh blue jeans and a designer polo shirt, neither was Dev. Where was the no-brand jacket and pulled-down baseball cap? The baggy clothing where he could hide the gun? "Dev, you have to explain."

"When we're in the car."

"Okay. I mean, I'm pretty hungry, so if it's lunch…"

It couldn't be lunch. You didn't kidnap someone to take them to lunch.

"Lunch is included."

"Good." She managed a skipping step to keep up with him, and almost fell.

He stopped. "Sorry, I'm going too fast."

"A little. Some people might say it's me going too slow."

He kind of gathered her against him, running his arm beneath hers and around her back, reaching up to settle her uncooperative left hand on his shoulder. Her whole body began to blur. That was how it felt. Blurry and fuzzy and soft. Happy. Her mind was racing but her body was happy, where it belonged.

His hip pressed into her side and DJ in the front carrier was right there with her little leg flapping against Jodie's stomach. Her hat was about to fall off. Jodie made an ineffective reaching movement with her right hand, and Dev saw what was happening and flipped the darling little pink-flowered bucket back into place.

"Let's not go slow, if we can help it," Dev said, in the corridor, and she could feel the vibration of his voice against her ribs. "Elin's probably sending out an APB, as we speak."

"So I'm right." She'd gone breathless, could he hear? "You are kidnapping me?"

"Yep, me and DJ."

"Oh, she's in on it?"

"Joint criminal masterminds, the two of us."

"That's a relief. I was scared she might be the hostage."

He turned serious suddenly. "Never, Jodie. I promise you that. I'll never try to use her as any kind of weapon or leverage or— But I think we really need to do this."

"I—I think so, too. Whatever it is."

"Thank you." He lost a little of the gun-to-the-hostage's-head feeling, and they walked together, in step, with DJ making sounds against his front and it just went on feeling way too nice, a complication Jodie didn't need when there was so much else to work out.

"Can I ask what it is?" she managed to ask.

"We're not telling you till we're on the road, are we, little pink person?"

"DJ, you'll tell me, won't you?" she said to the baby.

But DJ wouldn't spill.

Dev's car was parked in the visitor spaces out front. The day was bright and sunny and hot, and the effect of the air-conditioning had worn off during the time it had taken him to come into the rehab facility and collect her, so he opened all the doors to vent the hot air before strapping DJ back into her car carrier.

Jodie stood waiting and watching. She couldn't do that yet, the bending with DJ in her arms, the adjustment of the little body in the carrier, the fiddly, fine-motor-control-requiring snap together of the safety straps. He straightened and closed the car door. "Need some help getting in?"

But this she could manage on her own.

He went around to the driver's side, started the engine and the air-conditioning and they swung out of the parking lot and into the street.

"Now explain," she said. "You're not taking me to Oakbank behind my family's back?"

"Would that be terrible?"

"I— They're driving me crazy, if you want the truth, but they're doing so much to help. I hated that Mom and Lisa just showed up like that yesterday. It ruined the moment—"

"You got that right."

"—but it's because they care."

"Starting to wish they cared a little less. Or thought a little more."

"So we're not going to Oakbank?"

"Nope, although we can go visit horses at some point, if you want."

"At some point? What is this, Dev? Trish approves, I could see that. She was arguing with Elin back there and going blue in the face about it. Do Mom and Dad and my sisters know?"

"Your dad does. I talked to him last night. He packed your bag for you."

"Mmm, that might be interesting..."

"I gave him a list. He said he hadn't had any trouble with it."

"That might be even more interesting."

"Your mom and Lisa must know by now, because Elin would have told them the second Trish finished explaining. But your dad agreed it was best to keep quiet till we swung into action. Of course you can tell them, as soon as you want. Call them," he suggested, "once we're fully on the road."

It wouldn't be long. The car swooped between the traffic lights, made a tidy right and a wide left. Another two minutes and they'd be out of town. Jodie felt a surge of exhilaration and freedom that she hadn't had since before the accident. It was such a familiar feeling, yet distant somehow, because she hadn't had it for a long time. It was like urging Irish into a gallop across a wide green field, scary and wild and wonderful. Free, yet not alone. In control of something stronger than you were yourself.

"Yesterday was— I am not having that happen again," Dev said. "And even to find Elin there with you this morning. I appreciate she wants to support your therapy, but yet again, it turned everything into a big deal when it shouldn't be. That's why you need this. We both do. DJ does."

"You mean it really is a kidnapping?" She began to laugh. "You're not giving me back? There's not even a ransom note?"

"Not for at least a week. We need some time on our own, the three of us—I've found a cabin, made a reservation—and this is the only way it's going to happen."

"So you haven't even given them an address?"

"When I talked to Trish about it, she could see how important it was, and she's happy to have you take a break from rehab for a week or so, since you're tiring yourself out trying to make progress. She has the address."

"But she'll only hand it over once there's five million dollars in unmarked bills deposited in a locker at the bus station."

"You're really getting into this kidnapping idea."

"Yep."

He thought for a moment, then laughed. "Me, too."

They hit the highway and he sped up. DJ lay quiet in her seat. Jodie turned to look at her and found her kicking her feet in her tiny pink cotton shoes as if she were getting into the kidnapping idea, too. She smiled at the baby. *Hello, sweetheart.* But the smile was self-conscious and she wasn't surprised when DJ didn't smile back.

You can't make it happen, Jodie. Just give it time.

"Can I be the one to fire the gun from the car window to blow out Elin's tires when she comes after us?"

"Sure, since you've decided you're in on this, too."

"What should it be? A rifle? A sawed-off shotgun? I'm not real clued in on weaponry."

"Me, neither. But let's go for total overkill and make it an AK-47. You'll find it on the backseat next to your daughter."

She laughed again, then thought...daughter...mom. "What's my mother going to think? She's not going to let it rest with Dad."

"Your dad sees and knows more than he lets on. And he's strong-minded, when he wants to be."

"Oh, you noticed that, too?"

"He'll handle her."

"He will." Once more, she laughed. "He sure will!"

Dev pulled off the road at a shaded picnic area where there were wooden tables with bench seats and playground equipment and a picturesque pond with a viewing platform for spotting turtles and water birds. He'd brought a simple lunch of sub-style sandwiches and cartons of juice, and DJ watched them eat it from a commanding position in her car carrier, resting on top of the table. Dev cooed at her and she batted her hands for him and broke into the most dazzling smile.

So I do get to see her smile, even if it's not smiling for me, Jodie thought. "It's so quiet," she said out loud, because the smiling thought was painful despite how sensible she tried to be. "I love the quiet."

"Yeah, no phone calls, so far."

"They're probably running hot, back in town."

He packed up the picnic things, strapped DJ back in the car and they set off again, zoomed along in their bubble of air-conditioning, changed from highway to county road and the bends beckoned like a movie's happy ending, and DJ, without a care in the world, fell sound asleep.

Chapter Ten

Dev buzzed with victory and optimism the whole drive. To tweak Jodie's kidnapping comparison a little, he felt as if he were driving the getaway car after a billion-dollar heist. Yes, he had the precious cargo right here with him, and there was no one on his tail and he owned the world.

Almost four weeks ago, he'd told Jodie that the three of them were a family. Now at last they might have a chance at working out what that meant, the way he'd wanted from the beginning. He was a lawyer. He liked to know where he stood. He liked the ground rules in place.

Most importantly, he had a deep-seated need to see Jodie being a mother. Something would have to fall into place then, wouldn't it? She would find out what she wanted. She'd talk about it. They would come up with their own much simpler version of Barb's ridiculous spreadsheets, and if they could present a united front, then the three Palmer women would surely step back and give them some space.

He accepted that he wouldn't get to have DJ under his own roof, long-term, as much as his heart wanted, but he thought—or told himself—that he could deal with this as long as everything was amicable and settled. He'd *have* to deal with it.

It might even be pretty nice, down the track. He pictured a tomboy of an eight-year-old girl arriving at his place for regular visits with a purple backpack full of stuff. He saw himself on the phone with Jodie, negotiating in a friendly, casual way over what each of them would give DJ for her birthday and which of them would get to have her for Thanksgiving and Christmas. He saw himself returning from consultancy work in Asia or Europe with exotic trinkets for his daughter and her mom.

Braking to a halt in front of the cabin, it struck him that this picture was a little too simplified and idyllic to be plausible. DJ would probably acquire a stepfather at some point, for example. Jodie was too amazing to spend her life without a loving partner, if she wanted one.

And would Dev always buy those exotic trinkets himself, or would there be another woman in the picture with him, tolerating his absorption in his growing daughter, for the sake of a short-term sizzling affair?

New York was ten-hour's drive from Leighville. London and Hong Kong were a heck of lot farther. Right now, twenty-four hours without seeing DJ seemed like too long. What made him think it was going to get easier? What would happen if Jodie's bond with DJ became so strong that his own role ceased to matter?

The sense of victory ebbed like water out of a bath, but he pushed the doubts and questions aside. He'd been told the keys to the cabin would be waiting for them, beneath a flowerpot containing a red geranium beside the front door, and he could see the geranium from here.

Jodie stirred herself beside him. She hadn't been sleeping but she'd been very quiet, almost dreamy, and had now been roused by the dying of the engine. "So this is it?"

"Take your time. DJ's asleep. I'll bring in our stuff."

"Okay. Might grab a drink of water." She stretched in the passenger seat and found the water bottle he'd given her earlier.

Dev hit the trunk catch and brought out his bags and the cooler and boxes he'd packed with food. Jodie had opened the car door and pivoted to stretch her legs down to the ground. She was sipping on the water, looking around, apparently liking what she saw. She stood up and pushed all the car doors wide to give DJ plenty of fresh air while she slept. With the car parked right in front of the house in the shade and the whole place quiet and secluded, it would be perfectly safe to keep her there until she woke up on her own. Jodie bent to brush her cheek with one soft finger, then began to walk toward the cabin, a soft smile on her face as she took in the peaceful setting.

I've done the right thing, Dev decided. The only thing.

The place was beautiful, more like a log home than a cabin, larger than they really needed, only a few months old and built by the people who farmed this land to rent out for family vacations. It was also adjacent to a state park. He'd found it on the internet, looked at the photos and the map, liked the high ceilings and huge stretches of double-glazed window, the loft bedroom upstairs that he could use, and the master bedroom downstairs for Jodie, so that she wouldn't have to climb up and down.

Behind the cabin was a huge stretch of forested state park, with walking trails and a lake for boating, while the view through those enormous windows took in rolling green farmland and a wide bowl of sky. Outside, there was a garden and a deck, a swing set and a barbecue, while inside he liked the huge open-plan kitchen and living area, with its big squishy tan leather sofas and clean-cut décor. There was even a bookshelf crammed with vacation reading, ranging from crime fiction to teen vampire novels to romance.

The only downside, made apparent before Jodie had even made it through the front door, was the cell phone reception.

It was wa-a-ay too good.

When Dev came out for a second load of gear, Jodie had her phone pressed to her ear and was seated on the wooden steps that led up to the deck. She hadn't even made it inside. "It's beautiful.… No, she's asleep.… Plenty of space, it looks huge… Do? Does it matter what we do…? No, please don't call that often, Mom, you'll only get frustrated.… Why? Because I'm switching it off!"

She slid the phone shut with a click, stuffed it into her bag, looked up at Dev and gave him an upside-down smile, which he read like a book and reflected right back to her.

Families.

It's so great to be here.

Oh, you understand? Perfect.

They should be looking away from each other at this point. It had gone on for too long, and it was dangerous, after the massive flare of heat between them two nights ago. But he couldn't do anything about it, he just kept looking.

She leaned her head against one of the sturdy verticals of the deck railing, while Dev had stopped with his hand holding the door. His breath caught in his chest at the sight of that amazing, contradictory Jodie package. The strong will. The petite body. The forgiveness toward her family. The stubborn, triumphant action with the phone. The failed bond with her baby that his head understood the reasons for, while his heart just couldn't get at all.

Then she raised her arms in the air and deliberately broke the moment with a goofy grin and an exuberant yell, that echoed into the forest. "Woo-hoo!"

How was he going to keep from touching her? He'd promised Elin and himself that he wouldn't, but how? How was he going to make this week work the way it needed to?

He had to tough it out, that was all, pure and simple, keep his focus and his priorities, and he thought that Jodie did, too.

She'd yelled too loud, Jodie soon realized. She'd woken the baby.

Which was probably a good thing.

Because if she and Dev were going to look at each other like that again anytime soon, she might just conclude that way too much interference from her mother and sisters was exactly what they both needed. She had so little willpower where Devlin Browne was concerned.

DJ began with a whimper and a snuffle, progressed to a short riff on her current favorite sound—

"eeaaaah"—and then began to cry, building to full volume in around forty-five seconds.

Dev just stood there.

Jodie looked at him, heart sinking, head a mess. Her sense of peace had vanished so fast.

By now, at home, there would already have been at least two pairs of feet hurrying across the grass, two voices cooing and two pairs of hands reaching out, neither of them hers. She would have seen DJ safe in someone's loving arms being soothed and settled, and possibly changed and fed and made to smile, before she'd even pretended to herself that she was getting up and going over, before she'd begun to wrestle with the frightening, horrible reality that she didn't want to.

But Dev just stood there. Daring her. Waiting her out.

Judging her how much? Seeing how much?

Seeing *everything*.

She could see the muscles bunched at his jaw and his fingers tightening against his palms. He wanted to go to DJ. But he wanted Jodie to go more. And he understood exactly how much she struggled with it. It shocked her that he knew what was in her heart. She felt naked and guilty and defiant and just miserable. Why had she thought going away, just the three of them, would be a good idea?

"Don't make it into a big deal," she blurted out.

"You're the one who's doing that."

"No, I—" She stopped. "Am I?"

"I can't stand to hear her cry, by the way."

"Are you angry?"

"Not at all. Can you stand it? Listen to her."

"Please, please don't make it into a big deal."

"I'm not."

It was true. He wasn't *making* it into a big deal, because it already was one, all on its own. Dev didn't need to do a thing. The problem was her.

"I'm afraid I'll let her fall."

"I won't let that happen." He moved a little closer, treading down the front steps to ground level as if to reassure her that he'd be close behind.

"I'm afraid she'll cry worse if I pick her up, because I'm not the one who's familiar and I want her to love me and I'm scared of what she can see and feel. She's never yet once— Dev, she's never—"

"Come on." He reached out and pulled her up, and she decided not to make the horrible confession. *She's never smiled at me.*

Oh, DJ was a mess already! No question of smiling now. Her face was red and screwed up and even though Dev had parked in the shade and they'd left all the doors open her fuzzy, dark little hairline was slicked down with sweat from the effort of her crying.

Jodie fumbled with the clips of the car carrier, hating the fact that her fingers were still so wrong. They gripped when they should be loosening, they wouldn't obey her at all. Dev had to step in. He had the straps undone and loosened and out of the way in a couple of economical movements, intending to help but only underlining Jodie's inadequacy in the process. How could she take care of a baby safely?

She slid her hands behind DJ's back and managed to lift her. "I'm sorry I'm so bad at this, sweetheart.…"

Sweet.

Heart.

She is, but I'm not feeling it. All I'm feeling is the fear. All I'm hearing is the sound of her cry, and it's so

*loud and piercing and desperate, and makes me feel
so helpless because I don't know how to make it stop.*

She couldn't even feel Dev, although she knew he
was right beside her. He was a pillar of rock, hard and
blind. She straightened with DJ in her arms, and the
baby was so wriggly and heavy. Jodie's disobedient left
hand made a claw on the little pink-clad back. "Are my
fingers digging in? Am I hurting her?" she asked in a
panic.

"No, you're fine. Your hand's a bit tense, but it's
okay." He covered her hand with his, eased the claw position into softness. "Can you carry her into the house?
Let me know the second you think you're losing it. She's
due for her bottle. She wasn't ready for it when we had
our lunch but now she's probably crying from hunger,
so let's just head right for the couch."

"Can I get that far?"

"If you can't, I'm here. Try."

And she knew he was asking for much more than
simply making it to the couch.

So she tried.

*This is my baby. I love her. She's precious and tiny
and such a massive bundle of potential. Dev and I
made her. She's the two of us in combination, but she's
unique. She's dynamite. She might be president, some-
day. An Olympic champion, a world-famous musician, a
beloved wife. Beautiful and clever and kind and brave.*

*Who are you, DJ? When will you stop crying? When
will you smile at me?*

They climbed the steps. The cabin was cool inside,
shaded by the nearby woods, its screened windows
thrown open so that the breeze came right through. The
place was so new it still smelled like cedar and pine.

Jodie reached the couch and sank into its softness.

Dev slid a pillow beneath her arm for DJ's head. She wasn't so frantic now, but still she was crying. The sound and movement of it consumed her whole body and she didn't even seem to know that she was cradled in someone's arms.

Her mother's arms.

"I have a bottle made up for her," Dev said. "It's in the diaper bag. She'll need it warmed up, but that'll only take a minute or two."

They seemed endless, those minutes. DJ's eyes were screwed tight with crying. Jodie tried smiling down at her. Babies smiled when they saw someone smiling at them. So far it hadn't worked for her and it wasn't going to work today. "I love you, precious girl," she said, wondering what punishment life had in store for a woman who lied to her own baby.

"Here," Dev finally said, handing her the cylinder of plastic, warmed to blood heat.

Jodie shoved it into DJ's mouth. Oh, she didn't mean to do that, but her muscles weren't cooperating and it just happened. The plastic circle that kept the rubber teat in place bumped hard against DJ's gums and the baby shrieked.

"Oh, no… Oh, no…" Jodie said.

"It's okay. Did you slip?"

"Yes."

"It's okay."

"I hurt her."

"She's forgotten about it already."

And she had. Her little pink mouth had closed around the teat and she knew exactly what to do. She sucked it and the bottle began to make a singing sound as it emptied. "Will she get gas?"

"Give her a break. Lift her onto your shoulder and pat her back. Can you do that?"

"I think so." Clumsy, but still. DJ gave a burp and then a big wobble. Jodie half expected her to start crying again but she didn't, and with Dev's help she was soon in that lovely cradle position again, crooked in Jodie's left arm, beneath her breast, ready to finish her liquid meal.

She slowed toward the end of it. She was getting sleepy again. Jodie thought about enlisting Dev's help to put her down in the bassinet he'd brought, but decided there was no hurry. Okay, so DJ hadn't smiled yet, but she wasn't crying. Okay, so there was no overwhelming wave of love like the one Jodie had caught such a short, lovely glimpse of in her own heart at Oakbank, but still, this felt… It felt…

Peaceful.

Unhurried.

Unpressured.

Worthwhile.

Maybe I'll close my eyes for a little, too…

She woke up when Dev took DJ gently from her arms. "How long was I—?"

"Half an hour or so."

"And you've been sitting there the whole time in case I let her fall."

"Not the whole time. I took out some insurance." He gestured to a big, soft nest of pillows laid out on the floor in front of the couch. "She wouldn't have gone far. So I did some unpacking, set up the kitchen. It's beautiful outside. Hot, but there's a breeze, and the woods are shady. Want to explore?"

DJ did. She was wide-awake, bouncing in her daddy's arms, a pink frenzy of energy. With a dexterity borne of experience, Dev strapped her into her little front pouch carrier, facing forward so she could see everything that was going on.

"I'd love to explore," Jodie told him. "Let me change out of this skirt, though."

Dev screwed up his face and said slowly, "Yeah, about that…"

She gave him a questioning look.

"Remember in the car when you questioned your dad's capabilities in the packing department?"

"Uh, yes, I do."

"Well, you'll see for yourself."

"You're scaring me now." She stood up and made her way to the bedroom at the back of the cabin that looked out onto the woods. It was a lovely room, spacious and clean-lined, with the greenery outside giving it a cool light.

Dev and DJ followed her into the room and she saw that he'd opened the suitcase Dad had packed for her, but had left it on the bed with the top flipped back and everything still in place inside. "Just so you don't check the contents and decide I sabotaged them," he said. "This is exactly the way he had it."

She looked at the tangle of garments in the crammed piece of luggage. "This is it? This is what he packed?"

"I gave him a list, remember? He told me he'd followed it."

She looked some more, dipped her hands into the tangle and pulled out a pair of scarlet pantyhose she'd once worn as a Moulin Rouge dancer to a fancy dress ball. "Can I ask what was on the list?"

"Underwear and socks, a swimsuit, something warm in case the nights chill down, a couple of outfits for going out, daywear, et cetera."

She rummaged a little more. "Well, okay, I guess it's all there."

She set everything out on the bed, while Dev and DJ watched. DJ seemed to love the color and movement.

Item one—what looked to be the entire contents of her underwear and sock drawer, and she'd had "tidy underwear drawer" on her to-do list for a good six months before the accident. She thought about apologizing for the number of bras, since Dev had been the one to lug the suitcase inside, but didn't want to call attention to it.

For some reason, he seemed to be smiling.

"Did, um, my family toss any of my stuff when they moved it out of the cottage at Oakbank?"

"You tell me. You seem to own forty pairs of socks now. How many did you own before?"

"What can I say? Horse people need a lot of socks." She turned back to the suitcase.

Item two—a chocolate-brown halter-neck bikini she hadn't worn in five years, because on vacation in Florida where she'd bought it, it hadn't seemed too skimpy, but in Ohio it definitely did. Well, at least it didn't weigh much.

No comment from Dev.

But he was still smiling. Or had it progressed to a grin at this point?

Item three—the huge, vibrantly colored and fringed silk-and-wool gypsy shawl was warm, for sure, and finely woven and beautiful, but she kept it hanging in her room more as a decoration than something to wear.

"Where'd that come from?" Dev asked.

"Lisa bought it for me when they went to Europe."

"I think DJ likes it." Facing out at his chest height,

she was kicking her legs and flapping her arms. Not smiling, but close.

Item four—the bridesmaid dresses from Maddy's and Lisa's weddings. Maddy had gone for a sophisticated look, and her bridesmaids had worn strapless gold-and-silver sheaths. Lisa had wanted a Victorian feel with a hint of burlesque, which for some reason added up to sage-green satin overlaid with black lace. DJ liked both of those, too.

Item five—a single summer top, one pair of shorts and some hiking boots. "Those will team great with the shawl once the sun goes down," Dev said.

"Well, as long as I color-coordinate the socks..." She'd reached the bottom of the suitcase. "There's no pajamas or shoes."

"Huh. Sorry. My bad." He spread his hands, but they were grinning at each other, because how could you not? The whole bed was a mess of fabric and balled socks.

"Or toothbrush or makeup."

"Those were meant to be covered by the et cetera."

"Not as far as Dad was concerned, apparently."

"I should have checked."

"Or brush or comb or shampoo." She looked helplessly at the mess and thought of Dad, Dev's coconspirator, his intentions so good and the result so...*not*. "It's too funny, Dev. I love it!"

"You do?" DJ jiggled her little legs some more, against his front.

"It's so Dad. It's— Mom and Elin would have packed perfectly and sensibly and used up three suitcases. Dad just wanted us to make a clean getaway and didn't think it through."

"The clean-getaway part was pretty important."

"Yep."

"So…shop first and then explore the place, or the other way around?"

"The other way around. I didn't come all this way to buy a toothbrush. Even the hospital gift shop had those."

"And dinner out tonight, I'm thinking. Some low-key kind of place where they won't hate us for bringing a baby."

"Is there any other kind of place in Southern Ohio? Not sure I'll be wearing either of those dresses, though."

They took an easy ramble around the cabin, finding the start of the trail through the woods, a bench for sitting and looking at the view over the rolling woods and farmlands, a stone birdbath, and a newly planted stretch of garden that would look fabulous in a few years, especially in spring when the dogwood trees came into their extravagant white and pink colors.

With the baby right in the thick of things against Dev's front, Jodie expected him to push her a little, the way he had earlier when she'd been crying in the car, but he didn't and she was thankful for that. She needed breathing space. She couldn't bear to rush, or push herself.

In case DJ felt her tension and doubt.

In case Dev guessed just how blocked and lost she was, and despised her for it.

"It's so peaceful here," she said, aware of him watching her too closely, as he sometimes did. Did he see as much as DJ? She mustn't let him see. "So beautiful."

Look at the beauty, Dev, don't look at me.

Beyond a field of tall corn, they could see the farmhouse belonging to this piece of land. Jodie wondered if they'd meet the owners during their stay. She'd like to thank them for this place. "We'll definitely be back," she would want to tell them, but she didn't know if that would be possible. Who was "we"? Herself and DJ? All three of them?

"Like it, then?" Dev asked.

"Very much."

"DJ seems pretty happy, too." Okay, that was a push from him. The baby dangled against his front, completely at home in that position.

Because Dev expected it—and because she knew he was right—Jodie said to her, as brightly as she could, "Are you happy, DJ? Are you having fun?" And DJ gazed back at her with those big, wise eyes and didn't smile.

Chapter Eleven

That night, as planned, they went to a family-style place where no one minded that DJ lay in her stroller right beside the table and sat on Dev's lap for her bottle, and where there was a change table in a space of its own adjacent to the bathroom. The place quickly filled up with groups of all sizes, parents and grandparents and kids, couples with toddlers, dads with daughters, moms with sons.

An older couple came past on the way to their table, while Dev and Jodie waited for their entrées, and paused when they saw the baby, back in her stroller and growing sleepy. "Oh, she's beautiful!" the woman said.

"I'm sorry," the woman's husband apologized, standing back a little. "She never can resist a baby."

"It's fine," Dev said. "We think she's pretty hard to resist, too."

Jodie smiled and nodded and felt so exposed.

"How old is she?" The woman turned instinctively to Jodie.

Because I'm the mom.

"I— She's—" Her mind went blank and she didn't have the right answer. Did she say four months? DJ looked too small for that. So did she explain right away that the baby was born early?

"Almost four months," Dev answered easily, before Jodie had solved the dilemma in her head. He'd met these kinds of questions before.

"She's tiny!"

He'd met this reaction before, also. His answer was as easy and cheerful as before. "Getting bigger as fast as she knows how."

"What's her name?"

"We call her DJ."

"Oh, but that's short for something, right? My niece is CJ, short for Caroline Jean."

"We haven't decided yet, so for the moment it's just DJ."

"You haven't decided? And she's four months old? Well, if that don't beat all!" The woman laughed, not unkindly but definitely in surprise, as if today's new parents were a mystery to her, in a cute sort of way.

Jodie said quickly, "I like DJ. I can't imagine calling her anything else."

"Well, she is adorable."

"You make a beautiful family," her husband said, and the couple moved on.

"You like DJ?" Dev echoed quietly, once they were out of earshot. He leaned a little closer across the table and she felt their complicated connection like honey melting over her.

"I do. It belongs to her now." She remembered that

shocking day four weeks ago when she'd found Dev at his front door with his crying daughter in his arms. "It's…how we were introduced."

He sat back again. "I'm sorry, it just worked out that way."

"You don't have to apologize."

"We do need to find something, though, or she'll get that woman's reaction about her initials for the rest of her life."

"Dani Jane," Jodie blurted out, because suddenly it seemed important for DJ to have a proper name, one that came from her mom, one that was chosen with joy, even if no one used it very often.

"Yeah?" The intent look came again, coupled with a spark deep in his eyes. "You want it to be Dani Jane?"

"I don't know where it came from. But I just had a feeling. It's kind of sassy and strong, as well as being feminine. It's not too big a step away from DJ. When she's older, it gives her some choices about what she calls herself."

"I like it. What do you think, baby girl?"

But DJ had fallen asleep and couldn't give an opinion. Their meal arrived, in the form of two steaming plates of home-style meat and vegetables—one meat loaf, one sirloin tips. The other adult diners were tucking into similarly hearty fare, while kids mostly had plates of nuggets and fries or spaghetti with meatballs. There were at least four high chairs in use, and lots of messy kid faces streaked in ketchup or sporting milk moustaches.

"We fit right in," Jodie said.

"Weird, huh?" He frowned, suddenly.

"Not so weird."

"Different, then."

"You don't like it?" All Jodie wanted right now was to fit in, to be a normal mom.

"Let's just say, I'm a little suspicious when I fit in too well."

"You're an outlaw at heart?"

"I like a little adventure, for sure."

"This gravy is an adventure, as far as I'm concerned. What is that?" She speared a dark blob.

"Mushroom, I'm pretty sure."

"Okay, not such an adventure. Well, but it is, actually. Just being here. When a few months ago I was… nowhere. Something strange happened at first, Dev, although it's ebbing now. Sometimes when I smelled or tasted or touched something, the sensation was so strong and new. The day of the barbecue, when Dad was cooking those onions. It was as if no one in the world had ever smelled fried onions before, and the ketchup, too. It was like discovering gravity or gold."

"I've had that feeling sometimes with DJ," he answered slowly. "I hadn't thought of it that way, but you're right. As if I'm the first person in the world ever to take care of a baby. Just the smell of her hair…"

"Adventures and experiences don't have to be big and splashy, do they? The tiniest moments can be precious, and so fresh they sparkle."

"That's true…" His eyes had gone smoky and thoughtful.

I just wish I could find those moments with our baby, she wanted to tell him. *I wish the smell of her hair would make me feel as if the whole world was new. I wish I could see her smile for me.*

Should she say it?

But she left it too long and the moment passed and she was too scared. It was good being here with Dev.

She couldn't bear to spoil it, couldn't stand the idea of seeing his face change if she said too much about what was and wasn't in her heart.

DJ stayed asleep for the whole of their meal but wakened and grew fussy as they drove back to the cabin. Dev could tell that Jodie was tired, she knew, and he gave her the kind of easy way out she'd come to expect from her mother and sisters, not from him.

"You need a good night's sleep. Find something to read from that shelf of books to lull you off, and I'll take care of DJ. She can sleep in my room upstairs, and that way we won't disturb you if we're up in the night."

She should have argued. A normal mom would. A normal mom would never have reached the point where her baby was four months old and she'd never yet wakened in the night to handle a feed or a diaper change. But she didn't want to argue. What if she did wake for DJ and couldn't get the baby to settle again? What if she ended up calling for Dev because nothing was working, including her left hand as she attempted a solo diaper change?

To hide her feelings, she teased, "I must have worked pretty hard today to get that kind of a break."

But he was very serious when he answered. "You did great today, Jodie. You named her."

"I—I guess I did. Must have really taken it out of me, because I'm wiped." Don't cry, Jodie. Don't let him see. Step back so he doesn't feel how close you are to the edge. "Thank you," she said, falling back on those very useful words, not even knowing what she was thanking him for, right now. "In that case, I'll see you in the morning."

For nearly an hour she lay in bed listening to the

sounds he made as he took care of DJ, settled her in her bassinet, then relaxed in the living area with music playing.

Aching for him.

Aching for herself and what she was missing.

Aching for DJ, who had the best dad in the world.

The baby had a good night, Dev said. They ate breakfast out on the deck, just cereal and fruit and coffee. Since it would be kind of useful to have a toothbrush and more than one pair of pants, they drove half an hour to a major store and picked up a few essentials. Jodie would have bought more, but DJ began to signal that she thought shopping was way overrated, so the one extra pair of shorts and a strappy tank would have to do.

After lunch and naps for both mom and baby, Dev suggested exploring the trail through the woods, and that sounded safe. A family thing to do. A time when the dad carried the baby in that little front pouch.

"Time to break out the new shorts, you mean?" she said, so that he wouldn't guess what she was thinking.

"Sounds like a plan."

He left her alone to change. She was getting faster at it, but Ole Lefty still made some of the movements a challenge at times. In ten minutes or so, she met him back in the living area and they left the cabin, found the start of the marked trail leading into the woods and lost themselves in the cool greenery.

They walked slowly, because that was all she could do, but the pace didn't matter. Side by side, Jodie could hold on to Dev when she needed to, and he seemed to have an instinct about that, turning a little whenever the terrain grew too uneven. There were simple wooden benches at intervals, really just two tree stumps with a

plank nailed across the top, but they gave her the chance
to sit and regroup, and meant that they could go farther.

There was a stream gurgling just out of sight, tanta-
lizing them with its delicious sounds. There were car-
dinals and warblers, and they saw a greenish-brown
salamander flick itself beneath a rock. The air had a
fresh, peaty smell and it was so peaceful and quiet, just
the sounds of water and leaves, their footfalls on the
mushy earth, and Dev talking to DJ about the things
they saw.

"See the cardinal? It's red. Look at it flashing
through the trees, baby girl."

Jodie felt shut out of his ease with the baby, even
though she was right by his side. How could he talk
to her like that, so unselfconscious about it, when DJ
couldn't possibly understand? Red? Cardinal? How old
would she have to be to learn colors and birds? She
looked so happy there against his front in her pink outfit, with his voice so familiar in her ears.

I'm jealous....

Jodie felt the painful, complicated twist of it and
hated herself. How could she ruin such a perfect afternoon with her own messed-up feelings? She'd thought
a walk in the woods would be so safe, but instead she
felt as if she'd walked into an ambush.

"She's a little young for the nature talk, isn't she,
Dev?" The sour twist of shame and disappointment
came out in her tone, despite her best efforts.

"I hate when I hear parents talking to kids as if
they're not really people," he answered easily, as if he
hadn't heard the tone. He must have.

"But you coo at her." Her throat was tight. She'd
cooed at DJ, too, but it felt as if she were acting a role
that she'd been cast in by mistake. Faking it. And badly.

Like last night, when she hadn't been able to answer a simple question about DJ's age.

"I coo at her," Dev said. "I talk to her, I sing to her, I even confess things to her, sometimes."

"Confess things?" What did Dev have to confess? He had become the most amazing father in such a short time. He was doing everything right, the way he always did, without making a big deal out of it in any way.

He mimicked himself. "Man, honey, I'm not so keen on this diaper change stuff. I'm hoping you'll potty train real early."

She gave an upside-down laugh, disappointed. "Oh, that kind of confession." She blinked fast, feeling the wash of tears.

"Why, what did you think?" He leaned a little, his shoulder giving a gentle, playful push against hers. He couldn't have seen the tears. She'd blinked them away. He mimicked again. "DJ, don't tell the cops, I wrapped the gun in a rag and buried it in the backyard under the red rose bush."

But she couldn't laugh about it. "Thank you for kidnapping me," she said, her voice even tighter, unsteady now.

"We're back to that?" He put his arm around her.

"I need this. I'm not getting it right yet. You're being…so patient. But I need it so much." She stopped and pressed her lips together. Could she tell him? A part of her wanted to hold it back. Because what would he think if he knew? But then the words just came. "I'm afraid I'll never get it right."

"Get it right?"

"The love. Loving her. Being her mom." She was crying now. "It was a bad start. But that shouldn't matter. Other mothers have bad starts. A difficult birth, or a baby in the NICU so they don't get to hold her right away. I don't know why it matters for me, what's gone wrong, why I can't feel it. Don't tell me I need professional help. I have a ton of that with the rehab, and it's great, Trish and Lesley are both amazing, but I don't need any more of it. I just couldn't bear to have a therapist teach me how to be a mom, no matter how sensitive and skilful and well-meant."

"Hey… Hey…" He half turned her to him and she buried her face against his shoulder so he wouldn't see just how much she was crying.

Oh, who was she kidding? He didn't need to see. He could feel.

Her shoulders were shaking and she couldn't make them stop. For a long time she just let herself cry about everything in the whole world. About the accident and Dev's suffering that night and the birth. About the struggle with her body and brain. About Mom and Dad and Elin and Lisa and Maddy caring so much but understanding so little. About Dev putting his high-flying career in New York on hold, whether temporary or permanent, so he could be DJ's dad.

Oh, and why not just throw in war and the environment and a few natural disasters at the same time, and cry about those, too? She couldn't remember when she'd cried this hard.

Finally she spoke again. "I love her." DJ made the third side of their triangle. She'd gone quiet now, against Dev's chest. "I must. I do." Those little legs had stopped jiggling. "But I can't feel it. That's the most awful thing, Dev, such a terrible thing." Of course Dev talked to DJ like a grown-up, because those big, swimmy eyes of hers seemed to be taking in every horrible word Jodie spoke, every sobbing gasp of breath. "You must hate me right now."

Both of you.

He said gently, "What, you think I didn't guess from the beginning that you were having problems?"

"I—I— Mom and Elin and Lisa keep telling me it's because of the rehab, because I get too tired."

He made an impatient sound.

"But you don't buy that idea...."

"Maybe they really think that," he said. "Or maybe they're in denial. Or maybe they want to go easy on you for the best reasons in the world."

"That's pretty pointless, when I can't go easy on myself."

"You have felt it, the love. You felt it on Thursday at Oakbank, when you had her sitting up in front of you."

"I— I did. It was so wonderful. Such a relief. But it didn't survive Mom and Lisa showing up, and yesterday I struggled so hard, and that's crazy, for it to be so fragile."

"So it's fragile, for now. Dressing yourself was fragile a few weeks ago. Before that, talking was fragile. Your brain and body got stronger."

"It's not my brain. It's my heart."

"Don't worry about your heart."

"How can you say that, when for you it's so easy."

He gave a snort of laughter. "Easy?"

"It is easy. You change her and feed her and bathe her and carry her around and all the time you just love her without even trying."

It was true.

So help them both, it was true.

Dev fought to find an answer, a reassurance that wouldn't be glib and wrong, but he couldn't find one.

Jodie was right. Against everything he would have predicted about himself a year ago, he found it so easy to love DJ, and he couldn't just tell her mom how to do it, step-by-step, not when she was crying and crying like this, when the difficult words she spoke were just temporary lulls in the storm of sobbing and tears. He thought that the crying was vital and necessary, and it had been a long time coming, he guessed.

Tell her how to do it?

First, kiss her darling forehead and blow a raspberry on her tummy....

No. They were both out of their depth. Everything seemed like a platitude.

Relax. It will happen.

The only thing he could think of, the only thing that seemed to make sense at the moment, was to give love and reassurance to Jodie, and hope she'd be able to pass it on. Love worked that way, didn't it? The more you gave, the more there was. DJ had taught him that, just as Jodie had taught him that adventures could happen in the tiniest sparkling moments. He was still thinking about that.

"So maybe you shouldn't try, either," he finally said. "Maybe you should let go, and forgive yourself, and have some trust."

"Mmm." She sniffed and he clapped a hand to the back pocket of his pants in search of the wad of clean tissues he kept in there for DJ's needs. Jodie mopped at her face and he led her back to the last bench they'd passed, about fifty yards along the track, and they sat.

Just sat.

Shoulders pressed together, bodies like magnets, hearts in tune.

She needed this.

"I think you've always worked for what you wanted, haven't you?" he said, after a while. "I remember when you were sixteen when we put on that play and you wanted to do the lighting. You didn't know anything about theater lighting, but you promised you'd learn, and you did. You worked so hard at it. You've worked so hard at your riding, worked to gain the management skills so you could run the whole stable."

"You remember the lighting?"

"I wanted a red spotlight for my big speech and you wouldn't give me one because you thought it was melodramatic. You argued with the director—I've forgotten her name—until she saw your point."

"And you've hated me for it ever since. I'm amazed you remember this."

"Haven't hated you. Got over my ego, discovered you were right and admired you for fighting. But I don't think you can fight and work in that same way to learn love. Love just…happens."

"How did it happen for you?"

"With DJ?"

"Yes. Tell me about it, Dev. You've told me about the birth and how much she weighed and how much oxygen she had to have and all of that. Tell me about you. Because you were there. And I wasn't."

So he told her. Because she was right, she wasn't there, and *of course* he needed to tell her, and he should have realized it weeks ago. Just like her family, he'd protected her too much. While he spoke, DJ sat in her little pouch against his chest and listened to the sound of his voice coming through his shirt until she fell asleep.

"Well, after the first shock of the blood test showing you were pregnant, it was a while before anything happened," he said. "They focused on getting you stable,

and I was pretty busy with getting the plates in my leg.
Then they did an ultrasound and I saw her. Saw the
beating of her heart."

"Oh, wow."

"I'm so stupid, they gave me pictures and I put them
away and there was too much else to think about and I
haven't shown them to you."

"It's okay. I'm picturing it now. I can see the real
pictures later. I want to."

"They did another ultrasound at twenty weeks and
I was so scared they'd find something was wrong with
her because of the accident, but everything was normal
and we could see she was a girl."

"So you knew she was a girl three months before she
was born."

"And you weren't there to talk about names with me.
And I didn't want to give her a name you turned out to
hate. So she has the two initials on her birth certificate.
We're allowed to change it officially later. The more I
think about Dani Jane, the more I like it."

"Thank you."

"No, thank you. You gave her her name. That's important. Maybe if—"

"You're skipping ahead. Don't. Please."

"I am. Sorry. The next thing that happened was seeing her move, watching your tummy rippling and kicking up. It was…hard…amazing. But hard."

"Hard, why?"

"For your mom and dad and sisters. They laid their
hands on your stomach and felt her kick, while you
weren't moving at all and we didn't know if you ever
would."

"Oh."

"It was… Yeah, the doctors weren't saying much

about your recovery at that point. Some encouraging signs with your scans and tests, but a long way to go."

"And did you, too?"

"Did I, what?"

"Put your hand on my stomach,"

"Once. It seemed— I wasn't sure that I had the right to. But your mom wanted me to."

They both sat and thought about this for a moment. Dev remembered it so vividly, but couldn't put it into words. Jodie with her eyes closed, never moving, with those high-tech mechanical guardians around her, the monitors and alarms and tubing. The cool weave of the white hospital sheet. It had grown warm to his touch. He'd thought the baby had stopped moving for the moment and that he was going to miss out. He couldn't feel anything. She was as still as her mom. But then...

A twitch. A flutter. And then an actual kick, two or three of them, hard little bumps against his hand.

And he believed that day, as they all did, that if the baby could move so vigorously then Jodie had to be functioning in there somewhere. She had to be making progress.

"Were Mom and Dad angry that I was pregnant?" she asked.

"Angry? Jodie, it was just about the only thing that got them through it. Something to hope for. A sign that your body was still working enough to grow a healthy new life. None of us ever once thought about the fact that it hadn't been planned. It felt as if it *was* planned, by something greater than ourselves."

"And what happened next?"

"Well, you opened your eyes." Could she hear the scratch in his voice? Could she see him blinking too much? "That was pretty exciting. We'd been talking to you all along. We did tell you about the accident and the baby, but you don't remember."

"Not at all. Not even an inkling."

"We stopped talking about the baby at some point, because the doctors thought it might be too confusing for you, too stressful, if you kind of half understood in the coma but couldn't speak or react."

"I don't remember opening my eyes."

"No, well, it didn't last long, the first few times. That was hard for your mom. She expected too much, too quickly. She kind of nagged you about it and got very frustrated and upset and had to back off."

"I can imagine."

"Then DJ put on a growth spurt and they didn't like the fact that you couldn't move. They were afraid the blood supply would be compromised. They started talking about inducing labor early, but it happened on its own. Your mom was sitting with you and she could see the contractions, the tightening. You grimaced when they happened, and we all got pretty excited about that, too."

"Were you there at the birth?"

"Yes, right there the whole time. It was a quick labor, only a few hours, I think I told you that. Dr. Forbes had me cut the cord. They had to get her stable, but within a few hours I was able to hold her. They had us skin-to-skin."

"Skin—? Both of you? You and DJ? You mean you had your shirt off?"

"Yes, and she was just in a diaper. They do it a lot, now. It helps the baby's breathing and heart rate. They've done studies. Preemie babies gain weight faster if they can have skin-to-skin contact with their mom or dad."

She was quiet for a little while, thinking about this, and then she asked, "Did I have her skin-to-skin with me?"

He had to clear his throat. "Yes, a couple of times, the first few days."

"Oh. Oh, wow. I think— I think— No, for a moment I thought I could remember it. But no. I don't think it's a memory, I think it's just— Why didn't they keep doing it?"

"You got an infection and you were very sick for a while, and it wasn't safe for DJ to be with you. She went home, and that was when you started to wake up, and you were so confused."

"Confused... Maybe I remember that, a little. I didn't like it."

"You moaned a lot and seemed very distressed for several days. They didn't know at that point if you had permanent brain damage, and they decided it would be best to keep the baby away."

"Oh, I wish that hadn't happened."

"We just didn't know at that point, you see, if you'd ever be able to take care of her, or even take in that she was yours. It's been a miracle, really. It's so amazing to see you now, walking in the woods, talking and laughing, when a few months ago... Don't beat yourself up, Jodie. About anything. You're amazing."

You're amazing....

Pull back, Dev. This is too strong. This isn't what she needs, or what you need, either.

They both knew it. Jodie eased away from the shoulder-to-shoulder contact, pressing her lips together, visibly fighting to steady her breath. "Thank you," she said. "I've said that about five thousand times since I came home. But this is the biggest. Thank you. I needed to hear all of that. It's hard. This dramatic life story that I don't remember. But it helps. It will help, I think."

She stood up and walked to the nearest tree. Her movement was unsteady and lopsided and Dev wanted to jump up and give her his arm but he held himself in place, tried to watch her without it being too obvious that he was concerned. They both needed some space.

She leaned on the tree, her good hand running up and down the smooth trunk, then pressed her forehead against it as if it could infuse her with strength. She was thinking about something, wrestling with it, trying to decide what to say. He could see it, didn't know whether to prompt her.

"Need to head back?" he asked.

"We'd better."

He checked his watch and found it was already five o'clock. DJ would be wanting another bottle soon, or a nap first if she wasn't hungry yet. Later they could give her a bath and put a blanket on the floor so she could have a kick and a play. He outlined the plan to Jodie. Would she leave it all to him? Maybe he shouldn't have responded so much to her fatigue last night.

She stood straight, and there were two bright spots of color in her cheeks. "I want to take care of her tonight," she said. "By myself."

Yes-ss!

But there was more, and it was important, he could see. The color flamed even higher and there was a glitter of courage and determination and stubbornness in her blue eyes, the same glitter he'd seen yesterday when she'd told Barb and Lisa that if she could never ride Irish again, then DJ would.

"Dev, I want to have her skin-to-skin, the way I did in the hospital but don't even remember. Could we do that?

There's a spa bath in the master bedroom. We could go in it together. I'd want you nearby in case I slipped. But when you said I'd had her against my bare stomach in the coma when I don't remember… I want to have that happen. Then maybe she'll— Maybe at last I'll get her to—" She stopped and took another shuddery breath. "I want to know how it feels."

Chapter Twelve

"Of course we can do that." His voice came out on a husky rasp. "Absolutely, we can do that. We'll put you both in the spa bath."

"That would be perfect. I—I'd love it."

Forget giving Jodie space, he couldn't help himself, he had to touch her. Because of the color in her cheeks and the brightness in her eyes. Because of the emotional roller coaster that was still taking her on the ride of both their lives. How could he not touch her?

Hand on her hair, brush of his mouth across her lips to say, *I'm proud of you, I know how hard all of this is, you're amazing.*

She responded briefly to his kiss and the magnetism between them would have kicked in as strongly as ever, if there hadn't been this one thing that was even more important.

"Help me get back to the cabin?" Her left hand had

gone into its crab shape on his arm. He was coming to love Ole Lefty, as she often called it, because it tried so hard and was so brave when it failed, clawing and unable to let go, as if a victim of its own determination. Like Jodie herself. "I've done too much walking, Dev. Too much of everything." She laughed. "Crying. Living."

He put his arm around her waist and she leaned against him and they didn't need to speak anymore. It was a slow journey. He could have kept reassuring her, she could have kept apologizing, but they didn't. They didn't need to. The apologies and reassurances were understood between them without words. If he hadn't had the baby against his front, he would have offered to carry her, even though he knew she would have refused.

"So, did I win? Where's my gold medal?" she said as they came up the steps. "What, last place? Oh, well…"

"Last place? Of course you won," he told her.

DJ had gone to sleep. He laid her in her bassinet in the living area, over near the kitchen area, with the curtains and slatted blinds pulled across to darken the room, and she didn't waken, just sighed and snuffled and went quiet. They both stood and watched her in the new dimness, her parents, tangled together by her very existence, helpless about it.

Suddenly, Jodie was crying again, apologizing for it. "I'm sorry. I don't know why."

"It's okay. It's okay." Dev felt a rush of very male inadequacy, coupled with an equally male need to make things okay.

Right now.

In one move.

But he'd already said everything he knew to say. Did she want words? What else was there?

Well, holding her. They were standing so close it would be very easy.

It *was* very easy. Just his arms and her shoulders, the bump of their hips, stillness as she sighed against him. It happened before he planned it, a familiar phenomenon where she was concerned.

And then it changed.

He couldn't have her in his arms like this without wanting her, no matter what his head told him about Elin's warning a few days ago and his own understanding of the emotional risk.

Risk? Wasn't everything already at risk? Would fighting this heat really help?

He couldn't see it, couldn't remember Elin's arguments, or his own. All he could think of was Jodie's sweet, fierce little body pressed against him, proving her womanhood. All he wanted to do was quiet those shaking shoulders with the touch of his mouth on hers.

He did it and her mouth was right there, seeking his, wanting it just as much. It began as a kiss, but they both knew it wouldn't stop there. He could feel her bare legs against his, sliding their warmth across the muscles of his thighs. Her collarbone was bare, too, and he kissed the little hollows above it, making her gasp.

They sank to the cool brown leather of the couch and she stretched her body out, her spine and shoulders against the couch back, her legs half beneath his. He tried to lift her top and she sat up again and peeled it off, her breasts pert and round in a coral-pink satin bra. "Can't manage the catch," she said. "I always twist it around...."

But he'd already reached behind her and flicked the

hooks. You just needed the right angle, and the right movement with your thumb. The straps dropped from her shoulders, he tossed the bra out of the way, and there were those breasts he loved. He buried his face between them, lifted their tender weight with his hands and heard her breathing change. She'd forgotten about her tears.

I'll make you forget everything, sweetheart.

It seemed so simple. He forgot why he'd ever thought it wasn't.

It seemed like an adventure, a sparkling jewel of a moment, and those moments were the best adventures of all.

"Stand up," he whispered.

"Can't. Remember that marathon I just ran?"

So he helped her, popped the fastening on her shorts, shimmied them down and then the scrap of cotton and lace beneath. He loved her hips, loved the way they rocked so neatly. He bracketed his hands at her waist, amazed by the shape of her, the curves and lines, that butt so soft and silky against his palms.

She tried to lift his shirt. "This is where it all comes apart, sadly. Ole Lefty doesn't want to do this."

"Ole Lefty can have plenty of help. Don't even have to ask." He pulled off his shirt and she sank her fingers into his chest, rougher than she'd intended, probably, but he didn't mind. Hell, he totally didn't mind. The roughness heightened the beautiful chaos of everything, the sense that he didn't know quite what would happen next, where she would touch him next, whether it would be light or hard, what her breathing might do.

He ripped at his jeans, took his briefs down with them and stepped out, his hardness blatantly apparent. She reached down and touched him there, cradled his weight and he ached, just ached, and the ache radiated outward, up to his hairline and down to his toes.

"I never understand this," she said. "Why it's so magical."

"Just is."

"For you, too?"

"Yes."

How? Why?

Wanting her at eighteen but letting it go because he thought there must be a million women out there he'd want in the same way. Which had never really happened. There'd always been something missing. He'd put it down to his own naïveté. He didn't believe that anymore.

Discovering her last year, and then the accident cutting it all short, never letting him reach the usual moment with a woman where he began to think about how it should end. A final dinner out? Jewelry? A phone call? It could never have ended like that with Jodie.

Discovering her again three nights ago and finding that nothing had changed. If anything, had only grown stronger because of the complexity of what bound them together and pushed them apart.

He'd never known anything like this.

She pushed him onto the couch and sank on top of him, looking down into his face, those neat breasts grazing his chest and pushing higher, the softness at the apex of her thighs making a warm, perfect nest for his throbbing arousal. "You have to understand that this might not be pretty," she said, echoing what he'd said to her the other night as they stood against the front of the car. She was more serious than he'd been with the words, shy and fierce at the same time. "You might have to—"

"I don't care what I have to do," he interrupted. "Hold you, or guide myself. Start over. Shift. Anything. We managed fine the other night."

"You had protection right there in your wallet, the other night."

"Have it right there in my wallet now."

"On the floor?"

"Let me get it."

"I have it." She stretched down, giving him the perfect opportunity to take in the shape of her butt, the delicious curvy paleness of it in the dim room. A minute—quite a long minute—later she slid higher on his body, wearing a triumphant grin, clutching a square packet.

"You do have it."

"You have no idea. A wallet? Wasn't easy."

"Proud of you."

"Are you?"

"You're amazing."

"You always say that...."

"Yeah, I do. Because it's true. But let's quit talking now...."

Oh, yeah, let's definitely quit talking. There's way too much else to do.

She was right, there were a couple of times when it wasn't pretty, but hell, as always it was beautiful, more beautiful than ever. She laughed when her body wouldn't cooperate, gasped and shuddered and sighed when it did. He held her, rolled her, eased her thighs apart, caressed the whole length of her as he heard the build and raggedness of her breathing.

Inside her, he almost let go within seconds, had to school himself back, let her catch up, and when she did she took him over the edge so fast he lost all sense of time and space, could only feel and cry out and breathe.

They went into a bit of role reversal after this. She was the one who fell asleep within seconds, while he lay there in her arms wondering how to make the universe stop right here in this moment forever. Wishing she would wake up so they could talk and kiss. Glad that she didn't, because it meant he could watch her sleeping with his hand resting across her breasts. Wondering what would happen next.

He was scared of how important this felt, of what an adventure it might be, scared of this strange, vulnerable feeling that he couldn't really find a name for, didn't know what to do about it.

DJ was waking up. He heard the creak of her bassinet, the sound of a snuffle and the beginning of a cry. If she woke Jodie...

He eased himself away from her and she didn't stir. In the bedroom, some of Bill's chaotic wardrobe decisions littered the bed after Jodie's attempts to find something to wear this morning. He swept them aside, back into the suitcase, folded the sheet and quilt aside, then went and gathered Jodie up from the couch.

She was so warm and relaxed. Would she stay asleep? She wanted to have her bath with DJ, her session of skin-to-skin, but she was too tired for that right now. She needed to stay asleep until her energy rebounded.

He caught this tiny moment in himself of wanting her to change her mind about the skin-to-skin idea. How much would it achieve, really? She'd seemed so hopeful about it, what if it ended up a huge disappointment? What if Jodie couldn't manage to hold the baby? What if DJ cried?

We can deal with all that, he thought. *I'm making an issue out of nothing. What's wrong with me?*

She murmured something and he told her, "Just carrying you to the bed."

"Mmm."

He tucked her beneath the sheet like a child, laid the gypsy shawl on top because the quilt would be too warm, then went to get DJ before she began to cry in earnest.

Jodie woke some time later to find Dev treading softly out of the bedroom. He turned when he heard her move. "Damn, I woke you up, coming to check on you."

"You didn't. I was ready. How long did I sleep?" She felt a little self-conscious about it, and about what had led up to it. Her fierceness. His acceptance. The fact that it had happened at all. The fact that it had happened *again.*

Are we dating, Dev?

"A good hour," he said. "DJ's had her bottle and she's raring to go." He was silent for a moment, then said, "Shall I run the bath now? Do you still want—?"

"That would be great. Of course I still want." Beneath the sheet she began some stretches and range of motion exercises to shake off the heavy blanket of sleep, while Dev made preparations. She could see him through the open bedroom door, adding a generous squirt of bath foam and a sachet of scented salts.

The spa bath sat in the corner of the master bathroom, directly beside the two huge windows. They were made of clear glass and looked onto a thick screen of greenery with a barely visible lattice screen beyond, so that in complete privacy and warmth you would nevertheless feel as if you were bathing in the open forest.

When the water had been running in for several minutes, she levered herself off the bed, took the gypsy shawl he'd spread over her, wrapped it around her body, and went to the doorway. "How are we going to do this?"

"Can you get in by yourself?" He looked at her in the shawl, his gaze running down and up again, hard to read. "Do you need help?"

"It shouldn't be a problem."

"It could be slippery," he warned.

"There are steps and handholds."

"So once you're in, I'll give her to you. I'll stay right close by."

"That's safest, I think."

He seemed relieved. "It'll only be lukewarm, so she doesn't overheat or burn. Might feel a little cool to you."

"It's a warm day. Cool is good." Funny, for a change she was the one reassuring him.

And yet they were both nervous. Or not so much nervous, but keyed up. Was that it?

It was a bath, she told herself. Just a bath. But it was important. Too important even to talk about, so they talked about the tiny practicalities. Did they have enough towels? Was there a diaper and a clean outfit ready for DJ when she came out? Did Jodie need a robe? *Were* there any robes? Ah, yes, thick luxurious ones made of white towelling, two of them, folded in a small closet tucked behind the bathroom door.

She still felt churned up over what they'd said to each other out in the woods. Her painful confession about the state of her love for DJ. His stories about the pregnancy and birth. Now, on top of their lovemaking, it was like the aftermath of a storm, with a renewed sense of calm and a ton of work to do to deal with the litter of damage.

No, *damage* was wrong..

This wasn't about damage anymore, it was about healing.

Did Dev think so? "I'll give you a minute," he said.

For her to let the gypsy shawl drop, he meant, and climb into the water.

She felt crazily self-conscious when he left the bathroom and closed the door, as self-conscious as if he'd just stood there watching. She'd put on some weight in the weeks since leaving the hospital. Her breasts and hips were a little rounder, which was good, as the enhanced curves masked movements that were clumsier and less gracefully athletic than they used to be.

An hour ago when they'd made love, she'd warned him seriously that it might not be pretty. It couldn't have been, with this body. How much had he taken in? Why did the idea of being naked in front of him now seem so much scarier than it had the other night, or just now? It shouldn't have been any different.

She'd just begun the climb into the tub when he called to her, "How's it going?" She heard a creak and a movement, as if he were about to come through the door.

Naked, she froze in place. She didn't want him to see her. The reaction didn't make sense but existed anyway. "Not breaking any world records on the timing," she called to him. "Just climbing in now."

"Tell me when you're ready."

She sank into the water, wondering if the thick, mounded expanse of white foam was deliberate on his part. If it was, she was grateful for it. Beneath the waterline, you couldn't see a thing. "Okay, I'm good."

He opened the door. "Comfortable?"

"It's perfect." She looked up at him. His expression was serious. Worried, even. Reluctant. Out of his depth. He didn't need to be. Not as far as her safety was concerned, anyhow, or DJ's. "There's this sloping section on the side that I can lean against, and a kind of step to prop my feet so I don't slip too far down in the water. I'll be able to hold her. It's so lovely and deep, I'm almost floating."

He had his hand on the door handle, motionless, and for some reason the whole world seemed to echo his attitude. Everything went still and quiet. Beneath the water, her body tingled. "Uh, nice bathroom," he said, pulling the words out of nowhere. "I mean, it's just right for this."

"I know." She tried not to notice his awkward attitude. "The big tub is perfect. It would have been difficult in a smaller one. Where is she?"

"In her bassinet, to give me a chance to set up."

"What's she doing? She's not asleep? Please say she's not. I—I want this to happen, Dev. I'm not feeling patient, right now."

"It's fine. Composing a sonata for creaking wicker and plastic rattle, I'm pretty sure. I'll go get her."

A minute later he was back with DJ, who was wide-awake and happy, gurgling and cooing. He gave her a big squeeze and a fierce kiss on her tummy, then laid her on the bed and took off her clothing and diaper. "What a kick you got there, baby girl," he crooned. "Daddy's little athlete, aren't you, sweet thing?" He picked her up and came into the bathroom, knelt on the tiled step, cleared his throat. "Ready?"

Jodie lifted her arms. "Ready," she whispered.
Ohh

DJ wriggled as she touched the water. Dev still held her firmly. She was tiny and soft and slippery, and she half floated as her little arms and chin came to rest on Jodie's front. She had no bottom whatsoever, just a series of creases and folds. "Got her?" he said.

"Yes. But stay."

"Of course I'm staying." Right there, he meant. He didn't move from beside the tub, just rested his forearms on the cold white porcelain and watched.

Watched, and belonged.

Ohh.

There were no words for it. DJ's little body. The warmth. The soft lapping of the water. The slipperiness. The tenderness. The way the water helped with Jodie's imperfect coordination and control.

"Can I...play with her, Dev?"

"Play with her?"

"Bob her around, float her from side to side. I mean, she's never been in a tub this big, has she?"

"Of course play with her." He was still watching closely, his hair getting damp with steam from the tub, his shirt wet from the splash of the baby's legs. "As long as the water doesn't get into her mouth."

So they bobbed around and floated from side to side, her little legs making trails in the foam. The foam began to melt away, which was good because then Jodie didn't worry so much about it getting in the baby's mouth and eyes, as Dev had warned.

"Oh, you're beautiful," she crooned. "You're so beautiful."

And something shifted and changed inside her. She let go of the doubt and fear and questions because the moment was too huge and didn't leave any room for those things. She slid DJ a little higher and those pink starfish hands grabbed at Jodie's skin and suddenly it came.

A smile.

A big, sweet, soft-lipped, toothless, beaming baby smile.

"Ohh," she crooned. "You're smiling. Oh, you darling girl! Why are you smiling? Mom says you never smile in the bath."

"Because you're right in there with her," Dev said, "and you're smiling right at her."

"But I've tried that before and it's never worked. She's never ever smiled at me till now. Oh, baby girl!" She just couldn't take her eyes away.

"Tried it." He slid closer, along the side of the tub. "That was the difference. Now you're not trying, you're not thinking about it, you're just smiling."

"Oh. Oh."

No words. Just kisses. On DJ's tender shoulders, her forehead, her wet baby hair, her chubby cheeks. Jodie cradled her against her shoulder and almost swam with her, floating around the generous-size spa tub, bobbing and bouncing DJ through the water.

The sense of rightness coursed through her with as much warmth and vitality as the blood in her veins. *Oh, my baby girl, oh, my sweet precious angel.* It was a part of her, this new feeling. It wasn't like the short-lived flicker of feeling that had come two days ago at Oakbank. That had only been a glimpse. This was real and powerful and bone-deep, an utter, beloved certainty.

The water was getting too cool. Dev turned on the faucet and a blast of warmth jetted in, bringing the temperature back up. They stayed in there until Jodie and DJ were both wrinkle-skinned and even then, as she lifted the baby to pass her to Dev, she didn't want to let her go.

"You can have her for now," she warned him, making it a tease so that she didn't cry instead. "But watch out, because I want her back as soon as I'm out of here." It had been so precious and wonderful. She felt as if she'd recaptured something she hadn't known until today had been lost.

And it would last, this time. She believed it. Knew it. Knew that the overwhelming sensation of love had been real and true and deep enough not to ebb or fade. It was what Dev had. It changed everything.

"Careful, she's so slippery," she told Dev, and there was a wet, drippy tangle of arms and movements as he bent down to take her.

"I've got her," he said gruffly. "I know she's slippery. It's fine." He captured her in the big, fluffy towel and dressed her in a fresh outfit—lilac, this time—right there on the glass vanity while Jodie lolled in the water and watched him with their daughter. When she was dressed, he stepped into the next room and laid her on the bed. Jodie heard the sound of pillows being plumped and settled to keep her safely in place. "That's the way," he sang to her. "Not going anywhere like that, are you, sweetheart angel?"

DJ cooed at him.

"Now let me pass you a towel," he said, back in the bathroom. "Do you need help getting up?"

"No, there's enough to hold on to." But she slipped at her first try and slid back into the tub, her feet squeaking across the porcelain. The water churned. She gritted her teeth. Why was it so hard? How did such a clumsy episode follow so quickly from some of the most precious moments of her life?

I won't let the clumsiness spoil what I feel, she vowed, and made another effort, pulling herself from the water and into the towel Dev had waiting for her. *I couldn't let it spoil that, because it was too strong.*

"Everything okay?" he said.

"Like a miracle. Oh, Dev, I can't tell you…I can't describe it. I can't even think about the difference it's already made."

"Good. Good. I'm so glad."

She thought he was going to kiss her. She was sure of it, after the way they'd made love so recently, after the emotion unleashed by her holding DJ in the bath. His eyes had pooled with glinting darkness, half-shielded by a sweep of lashes, his mouth was so soft, his lips had parted and he was looking at her. She swayed closer, and her hands loosened on the towel. It would drop to the floor in another moment, and she didn't care.

As long as Dev kissed her.

But it didn't happen.

He took a long, harsh breath and stepped back, pressing his lips together, turning his head. "Better not leave DJ on the bed for long," he said. "I'll put her on the floor, with her baby gym. Time to think about dinner, too. It's been a big day."

"A great day."

"Yes." He left, picking up the baby on his way out.

Wrapped in the towel in the steaming bathroom, Jodie felt abandoned and hated the ebbing of that glorious feeling of love and relief that had made her so complete and so happy just moments ago.

The change in his mood was as stark and apparent as the sun vanishing behind a dark cloud. The air felt colder. The light seemed different. It no longer streamed like gold through the thick greenery as it had when she'd first climbed into the bath. The sun had almost set, and the bath water had taken on a greenish tinge from the sachet of bath salts Dev had poured in.

There was no more foam, Jodie realized. She and DJ had stayed in the bath for so long that it had gradually disappeared, and she'd been so absorbed in the baby that she hadn't noticed.

Dev would have seen everything. Not just the shape of her body lying there, but the awkwardness of it in movement, and somehow this left her more naked and vulnerable than she'd been the other night when they'd made love, or just now on the couch, because both those times it had been dark, or at least dim, and their need for each other had wrapped both of them in a kind of protective blanket. She'd felt a lot of things, but she hadn't felt exposed.

Now, she did, because Dev's mood had changed so suddenly, it seemed, and this had to be the reason why.

Jodie took a long time to reappear. DJ had grown bored on her blanket, even with the baby gym positioned above her. There was only so much rattle-whacking a four-month-old could tolerate, apparently. Dev picked her up and propped her on his hip while he attempted to put oven fries on a baking tray, toss a salad and grill steaks with one hand.

He'd cooked that way before.

"Wouldn't put you in your bassinet even if I thought you'd stay happy there, would I, baby girl?" he murmured to her, heart lurching in his chest at the stark thought of losing her.

Not losing her.

He couldn't lose her.

Jodie wasn't like that. No matter how strongly her bond with the baby kicked in, today and in the future, she wouldn't punish him with it, would she?

Not deliberately. She surely wasn't like that.

But the punishment could happen anyway, because he wanted too much. He'd been kidding himself so stupidly right up until tonight, thinking through all these plans about shared custody and generous access, about making it work even when he was in New York or Europe, not understanding that the bond he had with DJ was so much stronger because the baby hadn't had the chance to build a bond with her mom.

Just now, in the bath, when they'd smiled at each other, gotten lost in each other for minutes on end, forgotten about him so completely, both of them, and then Jodie had seemed so glowing and different after she stepped out of the tub, so much freer and more full of life, he'd seen it in the look on her face, felt it in the way her body moved.

The shutting out.

Like the slamming of a prison door, with himself on one side and Jodie and DJ on the other.

He felt sick at himself, a miserable wreck of selfishness and blindness and jealousy. Did he *want* to see Jodie go on floundering the way she had been, purely so that she would leave the best of the parenting to him? That was horrible. He was appalled about it.

But he felt it anyway, this sense that he was shut out and that it was a conspiracy coming from both of them.

He didn't understand why it had such a grip on him or what it meant.

Couldn't do a damned thing about it.

Here she was, at last. She was wearing a pair of

stretchy cream long johns and a flowery camisole top—amongst the more useful contents of her underwear drawer, he guessed—and she was wrapped in the gypsy shawl her sister had given her, that he'd laid on the bed. Strangely enough, the outfit almost worked. "Cold?" he asked, pushing his dark, unwanted feelings aside.

"From the bath."

"Right. DJ felt cool, too. You'll both warm up soon."

"Mmm."

"Dinner's nearly on the table."

"Thank you."

"DJ won't last much longer. We can eat, then I'll put her in her sleep suit and give her her last bottle and she'll go down. Can usually count on a good eight hours after that. With luck it'll be getting light before she wakes up. That's mostly how it works with her now." He sounded as if he were giving a lecture, and knew it came from his need to assert his own role.

I'm the one who took her home from the hospital. I'm the one who saw the sonogram and felt her move in your belly, when you knew nothing about it.

He'd told Jodie all that stuff himself, just a few hours ago, and it had changed everything, along with DJ's smile and Jodie's tearful smile back, and now he wanted Jodie's glow to fade? He was despicable.

Despicable, and lost.

The steaks were almost done. She helped him serve up and they ate without saying a lot. He talked about what they might do tomorrow—go visit the nearby lake, go back to the store to fill more of those gaps in her dad's packing—but it was all on the surface and they both knew something was wrong.

"May I feed her and put her to bed?" Jodie asked, after she'd finished eating. "Would you mind?"

"Mind? You're the mom," he said stiffly. "And you've missed out on a lot. You don't have to ask."

"No. Right. I guess I don't. Thank you."

"Don't say that."

"Sorry, I didn't mean—"

"We can't go on thanking each other for the most mundane childcare tasks. How's that going to work?"

"It's not, I guess, but— Yeah, okay, I won't keep thanking you."

"Let me know if you need any help."

"I will."

He was worse than Elin and Barb. He left the rest of the dinner mess in the kitchen and hovered around in the open-plan living area, ears almost aching from the effort of listening. He could hear her talking to DJ as she changed the baby's diaper, not the same way that he talked to her, but *right,* all the same, not forced or self-conscious, and the thick knot of incomprehensible jealousy tightened inside him.

Chapter Thirteen

"Yes, I'm fine," Jodie said into her cell phone. "I keep telling you, Mom... No, I'm not going to keep it switched on, from now on. I'll call you once a day to tell you I'm fine, and that's it."

She stood out on the deck, with her left hand pressed awkwardly against her ear to block out distracting sounds, and she had her back to Dev, even though he could hear her quite clearly. Was she trying to block him out, also?

She listened some more, then said to her mother, "Well, we've been out to dinner, we've explored the woods, we've been shopping to replace all the things Dad forgot to pack for me, we've been to the lake and had a picnic, soaked up the sun, cooked a barbecue here on the deck..." She listened again. "Coming home? Dev told them a week when he made the reservation." She turned and looked at him. "We've only been here three nights."

Was that a question in her face? Did she want to leave sooner?

His gut twisted. Maybe for her, the purpose had been achieved, there was no more point to this, and she wanted to go home. He wouldn't blame her. He hadn't been the best company since that magical session between Jodie and DJ in the bath. Hell, he was trying!

But he was trying to protect himself at the same time. He was floundering and she had to know something was wrong. "It's up to you," he murmured. "If you want to leave sooner…"

"Only if you do," she answered quietly, with her hand over the phone. Her eyes had narrowed, intent on his response.

"I don't."

"Good." She turned her attention once more to her mother. "I'll call again tomorrow." She listened. "Mom, you don't need to know the exact details on how many exercises I'm doing, okay?" Another pause. "Listen, I'm ending the call now. I'm not hanging up on you or anything, but there's nothing more we need to say." She thumbed the phone off and put it down on the outdoor table.

"Only if you do," she repeated deliberately, fixing Dev with those blue eyes.

"I don't," he repeated back.

"So what's wrong?" She crossed the space between them and tried to touch him, but he eased away, as he'd been doing since Saturday night. He didn't trust himself, close to her, and there was this massive sense of risk and vulnerability crashing through him that he didn't understand.

"Nothing," he said. "Just giving us both some space."

Her expression turned fierce and she stuck out her jaw. "Was that a one-off, on the couch, then? A two-off, I guess I should say, counting the other night in Deer Pond Park coming home from the restaurant. Be honest. Tell me up front."

"Up front…"

"It's not so hard, is it? You were pretty good at it, last year, the up front stuff. You said straight out that you weren't in the market for anything long-term and I appreciated your honesty."

Maybe if I knew the answer, it wouldn't be hard. Out loud, he told her, "Just…not a good idea."

"Yeah, you keep saying that."

"Twice. I've said it twice."

"Once for each time. If we go for a third, I'll let you say it again." She put a hand on her hip, jutted her chin in a defiant grin and struck a sassy pose that he knew ran only skin-deep.

"Stop…" he almost begged.

Stop being so brave. Stop asking for answers I don't have.

"Oh, me? *I* should stop?" She glared at him.

"No, okay, you're right. That's not fair. It's just… This—coming here—is about you and DJ, isn't it, not about you and me? I don't want anything to get in the way of that. What you're finding together. It's so great. It's beautiful to see."

"Yes, it is." A smile lit up her face, a new kind of smile. "Thank you for making it happen."

"That's her now, waking up."

"Oh, it is? Yes, I can hear her. Yes."

Three days ago, he would have had to urge her, *blackmail* her, almost, into going to her baby. Now she was already on the way, eager and awkward, calling out as she went. "I hear you, baby girl. I'm coming."

It was exactly what he wanted, better than he could have hoped, and she wasn't using it to hurt him, she was still giving him all the time he could want with his baby girl, so why was it killing him like this? What was he so afraid of?

He needed action and answers, not this pointless self-questioning.

Jodie had left her cell phone on the table. His was in his pocket, switched off just as hers had been. He took it out. It felt cool and compact in his hand, a familiar symbol of certainty and control.

Touching the screen, he had his office in New York on the line within seconds, knowing he was kidding himself about what this would achieve, even while he heard his assistant's voice. "Catch me up, Angie," he told her. "Has there been any news from London on the consultancy?"

"Can you believe I changed your diaper and your outfit all by myself?" Jodie cooed to DJ. "Your daddy will be so proud."

I'm lying to her. Again.

He wouldn't be proud, he would be uncomfortable and reluctant, and if she told him, "I changed her all by myself," he would say all the right things, but underneath there would be this distance. "Space" he'd called it, just now.

It wasn't space.

It was withdrawal, shutting down.

And she got it.

Yeah, don't worry, she got it completely, even though he hadn't spelled it out.

Mission accomplished, as far as he was concerned. He'd taken her and DJ away from Mom and Lisa and Elin in order to strengthen their bond and deepen her love, and it had worked better than either of them could have hoped. She loved her baby girl, her Dani Jane, in a way she hadn't imagined possible just a few days ago, with none of that thick, ugly layer of self-doubt and fear and unfamiliarity that had held her back.

Which meant that now Dev was free.

He loved his daughter, and he never would have abandoned her to the distance of her mother and the overinvolvement of her Palmer grandmother and aunts, but now that Jodie had her bonding in place, he was free. He could put this "family" thing he talked about onto the same footing as so many other kids had—live with the mom, see the dad occasionally for visits and weekends, while the parents maintained a cordial relationship if the kid was lucky.

Visits, where? Would he go back to New York? Jodie's family always seemed to assume so. Her heart lurched and sank at the idea. It felt so wrong to think of them at such a distance from each other, all the complicated arrangements they would have to make to keep DJ in his life.

She didn't want arrangements. She wanted him

It was pretty simple, really.

She loved him.

She'd known last fall that he would break her heart when he left, whether they slept together or didn't. He would break her heart when he left now, and little DJ, who knew nothing about any of this, was powerless to help, because there was no way in the world that Jodie would ever use her as leverage or a weapon.

"Look at you, sweetheart," Jodie whispered to her.

"How can I keep you happy and safe? How can I keep you from guessing how much I'm hurting? I can't let him guess, either."

She picked the baby up, put her in her stroller because that was the safest way to move a baby when you weren't sure of the strength of your own arms, and wheeled her back out to the deck, hearing Dev on the phone as she approached.

"Yeah, very glad I called," he was saying. "Sorry I had it switched off. I was trying for some space, but I'll keep it on now in case anything else comes up. It's going to be a mess if we don't straighten it out.... Yes, please, make the reservation...." He was so absorbed in the conversation, he hadn't seen her. He was staring out at the woods, not seeing them, either. "Yes, for Wednesday, if you can, so I'm there for meetings Thursday and Friday... I can fly out of Columbus to Chicago and then over the Pole, or through New York if that connects better. Just let me know the schedule when you have it.... Okay, talk soon."

He flipped the phone into his pocket, turned and saw her with the stroller wheels resting against the threshold between the living area and the deck. "Something's come up," she said, so that he didn't have to say it. "And you need to get to London before the end of the week."

"Yes. If my assistant can get the right flights, I'll have to leave here tomorrow and I won't be back before Tuesday."

"Tuesday," she echoed.

"I can't leave you here on your own."

She took a deep breath, let go of the instant, aching sense of loss, tried to hold on to what she had, the wonderful new sense of motherhood and love. She didn't have Dev's love, but she had DJ's. "I don't have to be on my own. We have the cabin till Friday. Mom could come out, I expect, or Lisa and the kids. Keep me company. Help pack."

"That's a good idea," he said slowly. "It would be great if you and DJ could stay for the full week. The timing on this is—"

Tough.

And yet he seemed relieved, too, which she understood. He didn't want to be here anymore, and this gave him the perfect excuse.

"What time tomorrow?" she asked, as if everything was fine.

"Depends on the flights."

"She'll get back to you today?"

"Within an hour, I hope. I hate not knowing what's happening."

He didn't have to hate it for long. His assistant got back to him as promised, with details on confirmed flights. By eleven o'clock tomorrow morning, he would be gone.

Jodie called home and spoke to Mom, fighting her way through the usual overanxious questions about her well-being and the baby's until she could get to the point. "Something's come up, Mom, and Dev has to go to London."

"London?"

"For work."

"Well, I gathered that. For how long? When?"

"He's leaving tomorrow."

"So you're coming back?" Mom sounded relieved.

"Well, I'm hoping I don't have to. It's been wonderful here. That's really why I'm calling."

"You can't possibly stay there on your own. You're

not driving yet. There's so much you can't manage. You're not saying that Dev's taking the baby?"

"Mom, if you'd let me get a word in edgewise, I'm not saying I'd stay here on my own, I'm wondering if someone can come out and keep me company. You or Dad or—"

"Of course we can." She sounded eager, now that she'd grasped the situation. "Yes, we absolutely can, one of us at least. You don't have to say another word. We'll work it out. What time do we need to be there?"

"He has to leave by eleven."

"I'll get right on it. We'll work something out. Just leave your cell phone switched on."

"Nope, not doing that."

"Jodie…"

"Because you'll call me every five minutes to update. Send a text, if there's anything important."

"Jodie, honey…"

But she stayed stubborn, gave Mom the directions to the cabin, ended the call and switched off her phone.

Again, Dev seemed relieved. "Last dinner out?" he suggested.

"Sounds great."

Sounded so final.

Chapter Fourteen

Jodie was in the bathroom when she heard the sound of a car arriving at the cabin at ten-thirty the next morning. Dev had almost finished packing. DJ was asleep in her bassinet. She hurried out and almost tripped on one of the rugs in the living area. There was a flash of red, parked out front.

Elin.

Her heart sank. Elin was the bossy sister, the one most likely to lecture, the one bluntest when she disapproved. And Jodie was quite sure she'd find something to disapprove of today.

But they had a big hug anyhow, because they were sisters, and in the end bossiness and lectures and bluntness took second place.

"I was sure Mom would be the one to come," Jodie said, while Elin took her overnight bag from the trunk of the car.

"She would have, if I'd let her. We had a great fight about it, her and Lisa and me. I won."

"So I gather."

Elin put her hands on her hips in a pose that said she wanted answers. "What's gone wrong, honey?"

"Nothing." *Make it bright, Jodie, make it casual.* "It's just business. Dev has to be in London. Only for a week. Less, really. Six days."

"Right." If there was one thing Elin was good at, it was communicating that she had a lot more to say, by means of saying nothing at all.

They went inside and met Dev with his luggage, ready to go.

"So fill me in," Elin ordered both of them.

"Well, she has a proper name," Dev said.

"Oh, she does?"

"Dani Jane."

"Your idea?"

"Jodie's."

"Really, honey?" Elin turned to her, face suddenly lit up. "I like it. I love it."

"It feels good," Jodie said. "Although I can't imagine calling her anything but DJ most of the time."

Nobody spoke. The brief moment of harmony and happiness had gone.

Dev studied his watch as if the hands and numbers had all turned back to front. "I should get going." He snapped his mouth shut, then opened it again and growled, "I wish she wasn't asleep."

"She won't wake up if you kiss her," Jodie told him. For some reason, she needed his goodbye to DJ to be a good one.

Only a week, she kept telling herself. Only a week. Less.

But it felt so much more final than that.

Dev was treating it that way. He'd been silent and distant this morning, as if in spirit he was already on the flight, sitting in his business-class seat and opening his laptop, eager to get to work.

He'd said to her from the beginning that the three of them were a family—himself, her and DJ—but it didn't feel that way, right now. This felt like the breakup she'd dreaded last year, the no-strings, no-regrets goodbye she would have said to him—pretended to really mean— when he went back to New York, if the accident and the baby had never happened.

"Please keep your phone switched on," he said to her, as they stood together beside DJ's bassinet.

"Oh, you want Mom to bug me every five minutes?"

"No. So I can call. To see how things are going."

"You can trust me with her, Dev."

"Of course I can."

It was horrible. There was nothing she could safely say. He tossed his laptop in its carrier case onto the front seat and she realized she hadn't seen it when he unpacked on arriving here. Then, he'd had it in his suitcase, out of sight and out of mind. Now, it occupied Jodie's passenger seat, the prime position.

Replacing her.

Making his priorities clear.

He didn't even hug her in farewell, just let his arm trail briefly across her shoulders. "Take care." Gruff, not looking in her direction.

He drove off, she couldn't help watching him with helpless, miserable longing until the car disappeared behind a patch of thick green summer foliage, and then she had Elin to contend with.

"What was that about?" She was still watching down

the road, where every now and then a flash of color or light from his car would reappear.

"I— What?"

"Did you have a fight? Help me, here, Jodie!" She wheeled around, stepped closer, put her hands back on her hips in what was a classic Elin-wants-answers pose. "I can't work out if it's killing him to leave, or if he can't wait. Whichever, I should be mad as hell at him, right? Shoot, I am mad! I could kill him!"

"We didn't have a fight."

"Then what the heck is his problem? What is yours?"

"Elin, I can't take this right now." She closed her eyes, knowing the tears would squeeze through her lashes anyway, and Elin would see them. She waited for the onslaught of critical big-sister words, but they didn't come.

Until finally, quietly, "You're in love with him, aren't you?"

"Only took you a year to work it out, sis."

"A year?"

"Okay, twelve years. Since high school. Not that I've been pining that long, I only thought about him if I happened to see his parents, or in the holidays wondering if he was back for a visit and I might see him. I saw his brother once, and thought for a second, from the back, that it was him."

"Yeah, you haven't been pining at all."

Jodie ignored this. "But last year, when he came back to town, I knew then, and it went bone-deep in a heartbeat, and—"

"And because of the accident, last year seems like yesterday," Elin said, understanding. "And now you have a baby together, and you don't know if that's the best or the worst thing that could have happened. Ah, honey…"

Elin *understood!*

"Real clever strategy on my part, wasn't it?" Jodie said wearily. "Get pregnant, spend eight months in a coma. Ten points for imaginative variation on the shotgun wedding."

"You didn't get pregnant on purpose."

"No. Which is a plus, really. Since it clearly hasn't worked."

"Hasn't worked?"

"He left. Did you notice?"

"For a week. Less."

"Not just a week. His whole heart left. He left, in spirit, a good thirty-six hours ago. The trick with the departing car just now was only an illusion."

"What happened, honey? What changed?"

"Dani Jane smiled at me. For the first time." Even thinking about it, in the midst of her turmoil about Dev, brought a smile to her face. "And I suddenly discovered how to love her. Which I hadn't known before. Did you—? You must have seen. Or suspected."

"We were worried. We thought maybe you just needed more time with your therapy."

"It was more than that."

"We thought a whole lot of things. Jodie, I realize we've behaved like interfering witches, the whole family, but we didn't know. If you would ever wake up. If Dev would want DJ all to himself and we'd never have that part of you, that legacy. And then when you found out about her and it seemed you weren't bonding with her the way you should, we didn't want to make a big deal of it, in case that made things worse."

"Well, it turns out that was what he was waiting for.

The love. The bonding. So he could pull back, get on with his real life, and know DJ was safe and happy."

"Bull. *Bull!*" Elin challenged.

"What?"

"That's *not* what I saw in his face!" she almost shouted. "That's not what that weird, distant goodbye meant, just now, Jodie. He wouldn't do it like that, if you're right about his reasons and his feelings."

"How do you know, Elin?"

"Because I've seen him, remember?" Her voice softened. "I've seen the way he sat by your bed while you were in the coma. I've seen how he bonded with DJ from the moment she was born, how he did everything he needed to do for her without question or complaint, how he fought with Mom—and, yes, with me—over who should be her primary carer and when you should be told about what had happened."

"So…"

"I can't tell you exactly why he went off like that. I really can't. But I can tell you it's not because he's just been waiting all this time to dump the baby on you and get out. I've accused him of that. Lisa has. We…we had a talk after you came here, Jodie, and we both realized we've let our emotions and our fears dictate the pace too much. But we were wrong to say that to him, or to think it, that he wanted to dump her. He loves her. And whatever else is going on—there's something, there's more—I think you need to find out."

"Find out…"

"Call him." It wasn't a request, it was an order. She pulled out her cell phone, made one press and his number was right there. She pushed it into Jodie's hand and pushed the hand to the ear in time for Jodie to hear a recorded message. Switched off, or out of range.

"So we'll go after him," said the bossiest sister in the Palmer family.

"DJ is—"

"Asleep. So we'll wake her up. It's only the first baby whose sleep schedule is the most sacred thing in the family timetable, honey. Once you get to number two and three… She'll live."

"Wh-what exactly are we doing? Saying to him?"

The hands went back on the hips. "Well, have you *told* him? That you love him?"

"No."

"So we're telling him that."

Easy-peasy, Elin.

Elin had a baby carrier strapped in her backseat. Jodie realized just how much the whole family had stepped in to help with DJ, because Elin's own kids hadn't needed special car seats for years. It was frustrating as hell to have so much family interference, and she loved Elin for it this morning with her whole heart.

Elin flirted with the speed limit out as far as the county road and for several miles beyond. There was no sign of the back of Dev's car. He'd had too much of a head start.

Too much of a head start, but what was this dark blue vehicle coming toward them? Elin screamed to a halt on the shoulder, and the blue car halted also, on the other side.

Dev.

Elin's window slid smoothly down. "What did you forget, Dev?" Her hands weren't on her hips this time, but only because they were on the window and the wheel.

"Couple of things." He opened the car door.

Elin climbed out, also. "One big thing, I hope." She

met him in the middle of the road, both of them ignoring the possibility of traffic.

"Yeah, you could say that." He cleared his throat.

Jodie sank into the passenger seat. She wasn't a fearful sort of person, but she was scared right now.

Scared?

Okay, a person was allowed to be scared.

Giving in to it?

No, she *hated* when she let herself do that.

She began the awkward process of going to join them. Maybe the white line in the middle of a county road was the right place for family treaty negotiations, after all.

Elin seemed to have a pretty clear idea of what was going on. She reached out, pulled Jodie closer, sent her in Dev's direction with a commanding nudge. "She's in love with you, Dev," she announced. "And I damn well hope you feel the same. Talk to her. Work it out. I'll be back at the cabin with Dani Jane."

And then she left, screeching through a turn that curved across both sides of the shoulder and made Jodie glad about the regulations on safety for infants in cars.

"Sometimes I'm glad your family is so keen on babysitting," Dev said. He moved to the side of the road, where a line of young sycamore trees gave shade against the summer heat.

She followed him, found a tree trunk to put her hand against, because she wasn't convinced she could stand without support for much longer. "Helps when there are things to work out," she agreed carefully.

He had his gaze fixed on her face, as the sound of Elin's car receded. "What your sister said..." He broke off, swore beneath his breath. He looked like a soldier ready for hand-to-hand combat and she couldn't look away. "Shoot, it almost doesn't matter."

"Doesn't matter?"

"Doesn't make a difference," he explained, frustrated and impatient and bristling with things she couldn't read. "To me."

"Oh."

"Because even if she's wrong about what you feel, I'm stuck with this. I love you, Jodie. Love you. I'm sick at myself, it's killing me."

"Loving me is so...h-horrible?"

"Loving you is horrible when it makes me so scared there isn't any room for me in the mix. When I see you and DJ together and I think my role disappeared, evaporated, the second your bond with her kicked in. I have this horrible jealousy..."

"Of me?"

"No. Of her. I'm jealous of *her*." He stepped closer, close enough to touch, but then he didn't touch her. "Of my own baby. For earning your smile, for earning that soft look on your face that says you have all the answers and everything that matters. For having your arms around her and owning your whole heart." Finally, he touched her, ran his hands around her back, looked into her eyes with his mouth just a few inches from hers. "Jodie, I need you to look like that at me," he whispered. "I need you to feel like that about me. That I'm your world. Not instead of DJ, but as well as her. Both of us. Your world. If Elin's right... Is she right? Can you look like that at me?"

"Aren't I looking at you like that already?" she whispered. "Right now?" She brushed her mouth against his. "You are my world, Dev, you and DJ, and when you left just now and I thought you didn't want that... You always said it and I always believed you. You weren't looking for anything long-term. How could I trust that any of that had suddenly changed? I was so scared. I hate being scared. I always fight it."

"You don't need to be scared about this. You're the bravest person I know. You've showed me that love can be the best adventure in the world, if two people want it to be. It doesn't have to be safe and boring and a massive compromise. And if you'll marry me, we'll make a family for DJ and she'll be part of the adventure, too, and neither of us will be scared of losing her or fighting over her or any of that." He dropped his voice still lower. "Will you, Jodie?"

"Yes, oh, yes." Her body decided to have a say in things at this point, and her legs suddenly wouldn't hold her up. She fell against him and he laughed and it was the best thing that could have happened, because what choice did he have now but to kiss her?

A car went past.

And then another one.

And then two more.

"I guess you could call it brave and adventurous to say yes to a marriage proposal on the shoulder of a well-used road," Jodie teased him.

"Brave and adventurous to *make* a marriage proposal in that situation. Some might say foolish. You deserve roses and candles and champagne and a whole heap of romantic planning, and here I am doing it in the exact opposite way, with no planning at all, and maybe I deserve, 'Do it better and you might get a yes,' but it… just didn't pan out like that."

"What was it John Lennon said? You told me, Dev. 'Life is what happens to you when you're busy making other plans.' I love that it happened like this. Of course

I said yes. We seem to have a history of doing things in the wrong way."

"In our own way. The adventurous way. A family."

"Let's go back. I'm missing her already. And I want to tell Elin."

"Wish the cell phone reception wasn't so good. The whole family will know in about five minutes and it won't be our sweet secret."

"Cell phone…" The outside world intruded, as she thought about it. "You'll miss your flight."

"They can wait a day, in London. I'll be away five days instead of six. It'll still seem like five times too long."

"Oh, it will…"

"But for now, I'm spending the day with family. And the night with my future bride."

Chapter Fifteen

The day Jodie and Dev got married was one of the best days of her life. "Let's not wait," they'd said to each other, and so it happened on a sunny fall day when DJ was still only just learning to sit up, and when Jodie's progress down the aisle of the Palmer and Browne family church was still a little uneven and slow.

The day, Christmas Day, when she and Dev sat DJ on the rocking horse Dad had made for her, was heart-warming and amazing and wonderful.

The day the following spring when she rode Irish for the first time since the accident was pretty good, too. Her friend Bec had kept him in training and given him an hour's workout before the ride, so by the time Jodie climbed into the saddle in the indoor arena at Oakbank, he wasn't in the mood to mistake any of her awkward leg aids as the instruction to go into a full gallop. He nuzzled her after the ride as if to say, "I'm glad to have you back," and if a good part of his appreciation was because of the carrots she gave him, well, that was okay.

The day DJ said her first word—"hot"—the day she took her first steps, the day Dev and Jodie finally tore themselves away from their baby and flew off for a delayed honeymoon in Aruba, were mighty fine days, all of them.

But if you backed her against a brick wall and pointed a water pistol at her head and made her choose the number-one day, the very top, most memorable, wonderful, important day, after eighteen months of wedded bliss, would have to be the one where Jodie discovered that she couldn't stand the smell of ketchup anymore, when it had smelled so good during her rehab.

It was in spring, and DJ had celebrated her second birthday the previous week. She was energetic, happy and talking a mile a minute, even though only her mom and dad could work out what she was saying half the time.

She loved children's music DVDs and playing in the sandbox and petting the ponies at Oakbank. She loved story time and bath time and Daddy coming home. She loved spaghetti and ice cream and strawberries, but her favorite food of all—this month, anyhow—was hot dogs.

Which was where the ketchup came in.

Dani Jane liked ketchup on her hot dogs.

A lot.

"Mo-ore, Momm-eee."

"There's already a big squeeze on it, DJ, honey."

"More, plee-ecase?"

"Okay, one more squirt."

They were in the kitchen of their brand-new, log-cabin–style house on their brand-new twenty acres of land adjacent to Oakbank Stables, and Dev was due back from an overnight trip to New York that afternoon.

I can't wait, Jodie was thinking as she squeezed the ketchup bottle, and then she caught the smell of it full in her nostrils and almost threw up and she just knew.

It was a Palmer thing. Mom remembered it. Elin and Lisa had both complained of it. Maddy swore it was nonsense, and then had called Mom from Cincinnati in tears one day to say, "I put ketchup on my fries and then I couldn't even look at them let alone eat them, and I didn't dare hope after we'd been trying so long, but John went to the drugstore and bought a test and *I'm pregnant!*"

I'm pregnant.

DJ ate her hot dog with her mommy being somewhat less patient than usual about how long it took and how much mess there was to clean up. Her nap time should have followed her lunch and she seemed a little surprised when Mommy bundled her into the car and zoomed off down the road to the nearest drugstore.

Dev arrived home at four, when DJ was still sleeping thanks to the late start to her nap, and when Jodie hadn't been expecting him for another two hours. She heard his car and met him at the door. He pulled her into his arms before she could speak and kissed her, hungry and happy and so familiar. "Finished early," he said. "Raced to the airport and took an earlier flight. Glad I've put the international stuff on hold for another year or two. Couldn't wait to see you."

"Me, too. I've been trying to call you. You had your cell phone switched off, I thought you must still be in meetings… Dev, guess what?"

She told him.

He kissed her again, and she found that his face was

wet with tears. She pulled back a little, looked at his wet lashes and narrowed eyes and mouth pressed tight to contain what he felt, and melted at the sight of such a strong man in such a tender state. She took some of the moisture onto her fingertip and showed him. "Wh-why, Dev?"

"Do you have to ask?" he whispered. "Because you're *here*, this time."

"Here?"

"With DJ, you weren't. You weren't present at all, and we both missed out on so much because of it. To have you here, and healthy, and my beautiful wife… Don't you want to cry?"

"I cried the whole afternoon." And she was crying again, laughing and sniffing and feeling crazy happy and emotional at the same time. "I went back and smelled that ketchup bottle three more times just because I could."

He laughed. "There you go."

"Because you're right, and it's just how I felt, too. I wasn't here, for DJ. This time, I'm having two pregnancies in one, and no one is going to stop me."

It was truer than either of them knew. Better than either of them knew. Three weeks later, a routine scan in the dark and quiet of the obstetrician's office showed that in roughly seven months, she and Dev would become the proud and happy parents of twins.

* * * * *

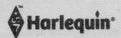
Harlequin®

COMING NEXT MONTH
Available August 30, 2011

SPECIAL EDITION

REQUEST YOUR FREE BOOKS!

2 FREE NOVELS PLUS 2 FREE GIFTS!

♠ Harlequin®

SPECIAL EDITION

Life, Love & Family

YES! Please send me 2 FREE Harlequin® Special Edition novels and my 2 FREE gifts (gifts are worth about $10). After receiving them, if I don't wish to receive any more books, I can return the shipping statement marked "cancel." If I don't cancel, I will receive 6 brand-new novels every month and be billed just $4.49 per book in the U.S. or $5.24 per book in Canada. That's a saving of at least 14% off the cover price! It's quite a bargain! Shipping and handling is just 50¢ per book in the U.S. and 75¢ per book in Canada.* I understand that accepting the 2 free books and gifts places me under no obligation to buy anything. I can always return a shipment and cancel at any time. Even if I never buy another book, the two free books and gifts are mine to keep forever.

235/335 HDN FEGF

Name _____ (PLEASE PRINT)

Address _____ Apt. #

City _____ State/Prov. _____ Zip/Postal Code

Signature (if under 18, a parent or guardian must sign)

Mail to the **Reader Service:**
IN U.S.A.: P.O. Box 1867, Buffalo, NY 14240-1867
IN CANADA: P.O. Box 609, Fort Erie, Ontario L2A 5X3

Not valid for current subscribers to Harlequin Special Edition books.

Want to try two free books from another line?
Call 1-800-873-8635 or visit www.ReaderService.com.

* Terms and prices subject to change without notice. Prices do not include applicable taxes. Sales tax applicable in N.Y. Canadian residents will be charged applicable taxes. Offer not valid in Quebec. This offer is limited to one order per household. All orders subject to credit approval. Credit or debit balances in a customer's account(s) may be offset by any other outstanding balance owed by or to the customer. Please allow 4 to 6 weeks for delivery. Offer available while quantities last.

Your Privacy—The Reader Service is committed to protecting your privacy. Our Privacy Policy is available online at www.ReaderService.com or upon request from the Reader Service.

We make a portion of our mailing list available to reputable third parties that offer products we believe may interest you. If you prefer that we not exchange your name with third parties, or if you wish to clarify or modify your communication preferences, please visit us at www.ReaderService.com/consumerschoice or write to us at Reader Service Preference Service, P.O. Box 9062, Buffalo, NY 14269. Include your complete name and address.

HSE11B

New York Times *and* USA TODAY *bestselling author*
Maya Banks presents a brand-new miniseries

PREGNANCY & PASSION

When four irresistible tycoons face
the consequences of temptation.

Book 1—ENTICED BY HIS FORGOTTEN LOVER

Available September 2011 from Harlequin® Desire®!

Rafael de Luca had been in bad situations before. A crowded ballroom could never make him sweat.

These people would never know that he had no memory of any of them.

He surveyed the party with grim tolerance, searching for the source of his unease.

At first his gaze flickered past her, but he yanked his attention back to a woman across the room. Her stare bored holes through him. Unflinching and steady, even when his eyes locked with hers.

Petite, even in heels, she had a creamy olive complexion. A wealth of inky-black curls cascaded over her shoulders and her eyes were equally dark.

She looked at him as if she'd already judged him and found him lacking. He'd never seen her before in his life. Or had he?

He cursed the gaping hole in his memory. He'd been diagnosed with selective amnesia after his accident four months ago. Which seemed like complete and utter bull. No one got amnesia except hysterical women in bad soap operas.

With a smile, he disengaged himself from the group

HDEXP0911

around him and made his way to the mystery woman.

She wasn't coy. She stared straight at him as he approached, her chin thrust upward in defiance.

"Excuse me, but have we met?" he asked in his smoothest voice.

His gaze moved over the generous swell of her breasts pushed up by the empire waist of her black cocktail dress.

When he glanced back up at her face, he saw fury in her eyes.

"Have we *met?*" Her voice was barely a whisper, but he felt each word like the crack of a whip.

Before he could process her response, she nailed him with a right hook. He stumbled back, holding his nose.

One of his guards stepped between Rafe and the woman, accidentally sending her to one knee. Her hand flew to the folds of her dress.

It was then, as she cupped her belly, that the realization hit him. She was pregnant.

Her eyes flashing, she turned and ran down the marble hallway.

Rafael ran after her. He burst from the hotel lobby, and saw two shoes sparkling in the moonlight, twinkling at him.

He blew out his breath in frustration and then shoved the pair of sparkly, ultrafeminine heels at his head of security.

"Find the woman who wore these shoes."

Will Rafael find his mystery woman?
Find out in Maya Banks's passionate new novel
ENTICED BY HIS FORGOTTEN LOVER
Available September 2011 from Harlequin® Desire®!

Harlequin Romance

Discover small-town warmth and community spirit in a brand-new trilogy from

PATRICIA THAYER

Where dreams are stitched...patch by patch!

Coming August 9, 2011.

Little Cowgirl Needs a Mom

Warm-spirited quilt shop owner Jenny Collins promises to help little Gracie finish the quilt her late mother started, even if it means butting heads with Gracie's father, grumpy but gorgeous rancher Evan Rafferty....

The Lonesome Rancher
(September 13, 2011)

Tall, Dark, Texas Ranger
(October 11, 2011)

HR17/45